ONE BULLET
TOO MANY

ONE BULLET TOO MANY

Paul Bennett

ROBERT HALE · LONDON

© Paul Bennett 2015
First published in Great Britain 2015

ISBN 978-0-7198-1621-5

Robert Hale Limited
Clerkenwell House
Clerkenwell Green
London EC1R 0HT

www.halebooks.com

2 4 6 8 10 9 7 5 3 1

Typeset in New Century Schoolbook
Printed in the UK by Berforts Information Press Ltd

Those who kill for pleasure are sadists. Those who kill for money are professionals. Those who kill for both are MERCENARIES.

War Dogs
Keith Cory-Jones

'Not all of us.'

Johnny Silver

PROLOGUE

Zimbabwe, Summer of 2000

WE WERE DRIVING in convoy, heading south along a dusty track that someone had ambitiously labelled a road on the map. The job didn't need all five of us, but we wanted to stick together. We had just completed a contract in the Balkans which had left a nasty taste in our mouths. We had been hired to end a dispute between what turned out to be two warlords, both as bad as each other. Having worked for one and given him a big advantage, we decided to join the other side and make things even again. We weren't just an ordinary bunch of mercenaries. We had morals. Money wasn't the only goal, but if we could earn some and keep a clear conscience at the same time, then that was all right by us. After all, you have to be able to look in the mirror each day and not be ashamed by what you see staring back at you.

I, Johnny Silver, leader of our group, was sitting beside Red, the half-Comanche Texan with jet-black hair blowing in the wind. He was driving a veteran Jeep that we hoped would last until we had crossed the border and were safely in South Africa. We had drawn lots for who would sit next to him and I had lost. Red's driving style was to have either the accelerator or brake pressed down hard onto the floor. He thought he was the best driver in the world and we knew he was the worst.

To the rear were blond-haired and baby-faced Pieter, the South African, and Stanislav the Pole, Stan the Man, Stan the Plan, our tactician and list-maker. When something needed doing, Stan came into his own – every detail had to be perfect for Stan. They were in a black Mercedes with our client, and his wife and son in the back. In the middle of the convoy was Bull, the Jamaican. He was coaxing an old truck, filled with the couple's most treasured possessions, to stay in between us and not become isolated and, therefore, unprotected.

Our client, Gunter Van Smidt, was a wealthy tobacco farmer in Masvingo province. *Was* being the operative word. Under the Mugabe regime, the white people were being forced out. It wasn't a peaceful transition: those who were not prepared to leave willingly and yield to a communist style of ownership were persuaded at gunpoint. It was go or be killed. Van Smidt had hung on as long as he could, hoping that the United Nations might step in and restore order. The best they were willing to do was impose sanctions on the Mugabe government. Now, with the natives arming themselves with Kalashnikovs courtesy of the Soviets, it was time for the family to call it a day, to flee and settle in South Africa.

We had been travelling since dawn and still had around 150 miles to go before we reached the border. On this sort of 'road', and bearing in mind the state of the truck, it would take us another five hours to complete the journey. The scenery was mostly veldt, some of it natural, some caused by deforestation, nearly all of it brown and dry from the continuing drought. There were fields of tobacco and maize, much of it rotting where the new owners hadn't quite got the hang of farming and the constant work that it involved. Every ten miles or so was a small village, mud huts on either side of the track we were travelling on. I could see one approaching in the distance.

A dog shot out of one of the huts and scampered across our path. Red slowed to let it get out of the way. Suddenly, an old woman with a walking stick stepped right in front of us. Red slammed on the brakes to avoid hitting her. She looked across at us and smiled.

I don't know what it was that alerted me, something unconscious like a small movement in one of the huts maybe, but it just didn't smell right. Instinctively, I shouted at Red.

'Back, back, get us back. Go!'

He was slamming the gear stick into reverse when the first bullets were fired. It was an ambush. We were caught in the crossfire. As the Jeep shot backwards, Red's foot right down to the floor, the first bullets hit us, sinking into the metal chassis. There was a cloud of dust coming from our wheels which helped to obscure us from the snipers. A hundred yards at high speed and Red brought the Jeep to a screaming halt. Behind us, the truck and the Mercedes stopped, too. Red and I grabbed our weapons and jumped out and ran to the back of the convoy. The five of us regrouped at the rear of the truck, hidden from view from those in the village. They looked at me for orders.

'We can't go round – the land is too rutted for the truck. The only thing to do is to take out the snipers.'

'How many do you reckon?' Bull asked.

'Two,' said Red.

'Too many bullets,' I said. 'I make it three. Two on the left and one on the right. Pieter, you stay here and guard the Smidts. Stan, get in the truck and give us cover. Bull, you and I go to the left; Red, you take the right.'

We turned our attention momentarily to our weapons. I checked that the Browning Hi-Power pistol was fully loaded and pushed it back in the holster on my belt. I took the Uzi in both hands and prepared for the assault. Both Red and Bull had AK47s – I'd never liked the Kalashnikovs because of the tendency to jam if not thoroughly treated with loving care. A seasoned campaigner loaded only twenty-seven bullets instead of the full twenty-eight that the magazine could hold – the last chamber empty to let all the dust and dirt sink to the bottom. Even then, give me the shorter, lighter Uzi any day.

Stan got into the truck and took it slowly forwards while keeping as low as possible in the cab. Bull, Red and I tucked ourselves at the back, waiting for the right time to break cover. As we cleared the first of the huts that formed the village, we jumped off, sprinted left and right and crouched down. Stan took the truck backwards to safety.

Bull and I worked our way along the village, kicking in doors and peering around them, our rifles at the ready. We heard a burst of fire coming from the other side of the road, and hoped that Red had got his man rather than the other way around.

We found our bushwhackers. They were both in the same hut. Stupid. They should have split up to increase the angle of fire on our convoy and to make it more difficult to get caught by a counter-attack. They were looking out of two windows, alerted by the shots that had rung out and expecting any danger to be in front of them. They spun round. We fired before they could react. At that distance a Kalashnikov can cut a man in half. Bull's target wasn't a pretty sight; mine was merely dead. We walked across to them and turned them over with our feet, still with rifles aimed at their hearts. It was an unnecessary precaution born of habit. I looked at Bull and shook my head, saddened to the core.

'Hell!' he said, staring down. 'What are they doing fighting wars?'

'Can't be more than fifteen years old,' I said. 'Should be in school, not mounting an ambush. How can they have so much hate at such a young age?'

'Must be the parents,' he said. 'I hope we come across them. They don't deserve to live.'

What you need to know about Bull is that he stands at six foot six, has a shaved head, is as black as ebony and his muscles rippled like a storm on the Atlantic. And, in his time, like the rest of us, had seen a lot of stuff you wanted to forget. He wasn't one to get emotional easily.

We walked back towards the truck. As Red emerged, I could see tears in his eyes.

'Were yours...?' he began.

'Yes,' I said. 'Just kids playing cowboys and Indians.'

'And they chose the wrong people as Indians,' Bull said.

'Let's get the hell out of here,' I said. 'Get this job finished.'

'Then we might be able to forget,' Red said.

'I doubt it,' I said. 'The image will haunt us for a long while. Makes a mockery of the old saying that only the good die young.'

'Can't turn back the clock,' Bull said. 'Life has to go on.'

Deep inside him, I knew he was as affected as Red and me by the incident. Even Red's hands were shaking as we neared the Jeep.

'You drive,' he said to me. 'Got some thinking to do.'

A few hours later, we dropped off Mr Smidt and his family and their possessions in the safety of South Africa. He offered us a bonus for killing the threats against them. None of us had the heart to take it. They had a new life before them; we merely had painful memories. We needed the break even more now.

And what did we learn from this? What was the moral? Expect the unexpected? No, too clichéd. Sentimental, maybe, but how about think hard about what you teach your children? Their first lesson may turn out to be their last. You shouldn't force your children to follow a path. Teach them right and wrong – that's enough. Then they'll always know what way to go. The straight path rather than the crooked.

I don't think any of us slept that night. I kept wondering who it was that had said 'only the good die young'. These boys weren't good, but they were playing a glorified game of war with live ammunition. A game where there was no shaking hands and going on your way afterwards. Maybe it should be 'only the bad die young'. Hell, I couldn't work it out. Can you?

CHAPTER ONE

The island of St Jude, Caribbean, the present day

A LOT HAD happened since the five of us had last met as a group in Texas to fight greed and prejudice. Anna and I were due to be married the next day and were waiting for our guests to arrive. They were booked into the five-star hotel that constituted pretty much all of the domestic product of the island. Anna was now six months pregnant and looking radiant. She was from Chechnya and had the classic bone structure of an Eastern European, and her face and body were bronzed by the sun. Her hair glinted with shades of blonde. Sometimes I would just stand there and stare at her, wondering just what I had done to be such a lucky man. It was to be our first child and we had built a new dwelling to house the soon-to-be three of us. It was just a simple bungalow, no glass in the windows so that it benefitted from the cooling effects of the light breeze that came from the sea, two bedrooms, a kitchen and bathroom. It was sited a hundred yards along the beach from the bar, which we ran and which gave the guests something a bit more native and with more colour than the sanitised facilities of the hotel.

Bull was to be my best man. He had a boat and ran fishing trips – the hotel guests regularly saw marlin fishing as one of the main attractions of staying on the island. That and the tranquillity – can't get enough tranquillity if one has been a mercenary.

Bull's wife, Mai Ling – an extraordinarily pretty woman whose roots were half Chinese and half African – would be maid of honour, or so I was told. I was short of knowledge in the marriage department so went along happily with what Anna decided was appropriate protocol.

Tonight, we would all assemble for a beach barbecue and celebrate our last night as single people. I wasn't quite sure how my mother would take to such informality, but hoped that a few rum punches and the convivial atmosphere of old friends and relations would see her entering into the mood. Maybe Uncle Gus, my biological father, would jolly her along – he was good at making people happy.

I was behind the bar, having served some cocktails to an American couple, when Bull walked over from his boat, limping slightly where he had been hamstrung by the Russians. My souvenir of that encounter was six bullets in the shoulder where they had ripped out much of the muscle. We made a fine pair.

'Tomorrow then,' he said.

'Yep.'

'Big step,' he said.

'Reckon so.'

'Any anxieties?'

'Apart from everything, no.'

'Good,' he said. 'Because it's my job to help you overcome them.'

'And you're doing a pretty good job. Before you arrived I had my nervousness under control.'

'Glad to be of service.' He smiled. 'Thirsty work being a best man. Beer would be good.'

I took two bottles of beer from the fridge, opened them and

passed one to him. I held the frosted bottle to my forehead to enjoy the coolness it brought, then took a sip.

'Lot of things can go wrong,' he said. 'I made a long list.'

'You're enjoying this, aren't you?'

'Maybe.'

'What do you mean "maybe"?'

'That's what you always say when we're in a tight spot. *Maybe* if we do such and such people will stop trying to kill us.'

'So it's payback time?'

He grinned at me. 'Every last bit of it.'

'I hate to ask this, but have you got the ring?'

'No, I threw it overboard to see if the fishes would bite.' He paused. 'Course I got the ring.' He took a long draught of his beer and nodded to himself with satisfaction. 'Relax, Johnny,' he said. 'Everything's organized down to the last detail.'

'Would Stan be happy with the arrangements?'

'Even Stan would.'

'Good enough for me, then.'

'Wonder what they've been up to?' he said. 'Pieter's predictable – he'll have been chasing skirt, or fending them off if what he says about his rich widow clients on safari is true.'

Pieter had got us into more fights than I cared to remember. He was an inveterate womaniser. A man's got to have some hobby, I suppose.

'Stan will have been building business at his hotel on some unpronounceable Polish lake,' I said. 'The whole thing will run like clockwork.'

'And Red will be getting his ranch in working order, if he hasn't sold up and taken the money and run.'

'He won't have sold up,' I said confidently. 'He's like all of us. The time for fighting other people's battles is over. The only thing to do is find a good woman and settle down. Hang

15

up your gun-belt for good.'

'Still got that Browning taped under the bar counter?'

'Still got that shotgun hidden in the engine compartment of your boat?' I countered.

'Old habits die hard,' he said.

'Don't make them bad, though.'

'Pays to be careful.'

'Reckon so.'

Gus, who arrived by helicopter with my mother – owning a merchant bank has its privileges – was the first to arrive for the beach party. This is complicated, but stick with me while I try to explain about Gus and me. Gus (full name Giuseppe Gordini) is technically my uncle – that is, he's the brother of the man (Alfredo Gordini) on my birth certificate as my father. But actually Gus is my biological father, although this secret is only known by Gus, my mother and myself. So, one half of me is American. My mother is English. The maternal line is Jewish and the paternal, Italian-American, side of the family is Catholic – makes for a pretty messed up child-hood. I told you it was complicated. I get my dark hair and colouring from Gus, along with his easy-going outlook on life. From my mother I get an intelligent and enquiring mind, a tall, lean figure, and a certain quality – if it can be called that – of stubbornness. When I think of Alfredo and my two brothers by him, Roberto and Carlo, I think I got the best of the genetic pool. Ah, but where do I get the eyes, the eyes of a mercenary – cold, dark pools that promise death? Maybe they were nurture rather than nature.

Today Gus – what we English would call a dapper dresser – was wearing a pair of navy blue slacks and a crisp, white short-sleeved shirt. His long silver hair had been cut since I had last seen him in Amsterdam and now just touched his ears. His brown eyes shone brightly. He smiled broadly and gave me a big hug.

'Thought you might need some help,' he said.

'Always welcome,' I said. 'Good to see you again. Been too long.'

'I hear you had some trouble down in Texas.'

'Nothing we couldn't handle.'

'So I hear. Close, though, they say.'

I nodded and frowned, thinking of the day I had to use my gun on this very spot.

He looked past me and gave an even bigger smile. I turned around and saw Anna walking along the beach. She was wearing a long, white flowing dress that caressed her ankles. She had on gold, flat-heeled sandals. Her hair was swept up and revealed two small pearl earrings. She looked a million dollars. Gus walked towards her, held her in his arms and kissed her on both cheeks. He released his hold and stepped back a pace.

'Great to see you,' he said. 'You look blooming. Pregnancy becomes you, my darling. Come, sit down, take the weight off your feet.'

'Don't you start, too. I have enough trouble with Johnny fussing over me. But thank you for the thought. Let me get you a drink.'

She walked up to the bar and went inside, took an ice-cold jug from the fridge, poured rum punch into two frosted glasses and handed one to Gus and one to me; for herself, tonic water. Gus raised his glass and toasted us.

'Here's to you both,' he said. 'And the one to come.'

I left Gus talking to Anna and went to examine the charcoal in the two half-oil drums that were serving as my barbecue. They were almost at the white heat stage when I should be putting the meat, and then the fish, on to cook.

17

Next to arrive was Tobias. He was another British immigrant to make the island his own. Retired from an oil company where he had been a surveyor, he had a small sailing vessel and spent his time exploring the coast around St Jude and the neighbouring islands. Tobias could be taken for a stunt double of Popeye the sailor man. He had a ruddy complexion from the sun and the wind burn while sailing, wore a peaked cap and seemed to be permanently sucking on a pipe.

'Thought you might like some help,' he said.

If it went on like this, I could delegate all my duties and sit back and relax.

'Kind of you to offer. The choice is fish or meat – barbecued, that is.'

'I'll take the fish – takes less time, which gives me more for drinking.'

'Good plan,' I said. 'Stan would approve – you'll meet him later. Forgive his wise sayings about pickled cucumbers and you'll get to like him.'

'I look forward to meeting any friend of yours,' he replied, knocking the ash from his pipe on the side of the bar and then placing the pipe in his pocket for after he had finished cooking.

I got the meat and fish out of the fridge, gave Gus and Tobias the implements they needed and handed the meat to Gus and the fish to Tobias. I poured Tobias a neat Jamaican rum – fittingly for an old sea dog, he would drink nothing else – and left them to it for a while. I checked the long table that we had hired from the hotel together with the starched dazzling white tablecloths. I set out bread and bowls of salad and repositioned the umbrellas to give a bit more shade. Later, we could roll them up for an uninterrupted view of the sun going down over the azure sea. Priceless.

A mere ten minutes later, everything was ready and keeping warm. Theoretically, I could now relax. But not before I had seen Mother and her reaction to Anna. Surely she would warm to her like everybody else? What was not to like, if Anna's history was not revealed? I had rescued her from the Russian masters who had forced her to ply the most ancient profession – of the highest class, though. Gus wouldn't have told my mother, so Anna could start with a clean sheet.

My mother was wearing a white trouser suit with silver sandals. Her grey hair was scraped back and held with two tortoiseshell combs.

'Is that Anna?' she asked.

I nodded. 'What do you think?'

'She is very beautiful.'

'And?'

'Would it matter what I think?'

'It wouldn't make a difference to the wedding, but it would matter to me.'

'Give us a chance to get to know each other. Introduce me.'

I took Mother across the platinum sand to where Anna was standing. I made the introductions.

'You can go now, Johnny,' Mother said. 'Time for girl talk.'

'But ...'

'Go! Shoo!' said Mother, making a waving motion with her fingers.

I looked across at Anna to read her reaction. She gave me a smile. I shrugged my shoulders and turned to look across the beach. A large group was walking along the sand. In front were my half-brother, Carlo, and his fiancée, Natasha. Natasha and Anna had the same history and, against the odds, had captivated two brothers from the same family. Behind them I could see the tall figure of Bull and the outlines against the sun of Red, Pieter and Stan. Red, half-Comanche, had long dark hair and was wearing stone-washed jeans, a white shirt and cowboy boots, just as if he stepped straight from his ranch in Texas. Maybe he had. Pieter had on a khaki safari suit and a wide brimmed hat which he took off as he walked and used to fan himself. Bull had with him Mai Ling and their little boy, Michael. White seemed to be the order of the day for the women as both Mai Ling and Natasha wore the same colour as Mother and Anna. Bull had on a light blue T-shirt that strained against his chest muscles and a pair of dark blue chinos. Stan stepped out of the light and into the shade. I could see him clearly now.

'Jesus!' I said. 'What happened to you?'

His face was a mess. Both eyes were black and the left one was heavily swollen. He had a large plaster across the bridge of his nose, a cut to his cheek and a thick lip doing an impression of a balloon.

'Walked into a door,' Stan said.

'Thank goodness for that. I thought you had slipped on a bar of soap.'

Stan tried to force a grin, but it was out of character and obviously painful, too.

'Well,' I said. 'What really happened?'

'Not now, Johnny. I'll tell you tomorrow, maybe.'

'No maybes about it. Can you manage a drink?'

'Have you got a straw?'

I nodded and walked to the bar, poured a rum punch and put a straw in it. I passed it to Stan and looked at Bull.

'Don't ask me,' he said. 'I'm as much in the dark as you. Tomorrow was all he said to me, too. Seems like we've got to wait to find out what he's keeping secret.'

'Wow,' Stan said. 'This is good. What's in it?'

'Rum and other stuff,' I said.

'What other stuff?'

'It's a secret recipe. If I told you, I'd have to kill you.'

'You just might be saving someone the trouble.'

It was like a black cloud descending on me and wrapping itself tightly around my body. Bull was at the bar and looking across at me. I'd known him too long not to read that look. I feel the same, he seemed to say.

I walked up to him and placed my glass of punch on the wooden top of the bar.

'Wrong drink for the circumstances,' he said.

I nodded and went behind the bar. Selected a bottle of premium high-strength vodka, placed ice in a highball glass and drizzled the vodka over so that I could savour that lovely sound of ice cracking with all the promise of what was to come. I passed the glass to Bull and repeated the process for myself. We stood there for a moment, not wanting to break the spell.

'It'll be bad,' Bull said. 'Whatever the story Stan tells us it will be bad. Bad for him and for us.'

'Yeah. He wouldn't have shown up otherwise. Just have made some excuse and hidden his wounds from us. He wants us to know, and you know what that means?'

'Trouble heading our way,' Bull said, downing his drink.

He pushed the glass back to me and I refilled it.

'By rights,' I said, 'we should be drinking mineral water. Keep a clear head.'

'Never worked for me in the past,' he said. 'Sometimes you need a big hit to jolt the system back into full working order.'

'Timing's not great, is it?' I said, letting my eyes roam to take in the guests filled with jollity.

'Always the same with you,' Bull said, shaking his head. 'Trouble only just around the corner. Sticks its head round

21

and says "peek-a-boo".'

'Peek-a-boo?' I said.

'Best I could do with all these ladies present. However you want to phrase it, it's going to end up in a fight. I know it and you know it, too. This is how it starts, and then finishes with shots bouncing all around.'

'Maybe it will be different this time.'

'Maybe, brother. Maybe.'

The steel band struck up and started to play 'Yellow Bird'. My mother, uncharacteristically giggling, grabbed Gus's hand and dragged him up on to the small clearing in the sand. Somehow, and to the mystification of the other guests, they managed to waltz to the reggae rhythm. It raised the mood by at least two notches and others now rose from the tables and joined them. Anna looked across at me and beckoned with her little finger. I walked across to her. Henpecked? Who me?

'Dance with me,' she said.

'But … ' I began.

'No excuses,' she said. 'If your mother can dance, then so can you.'

'But I don't dance.'

'You do now.'

Resigned to my fate, I took her hand and we joined the other couples. The band slowed the tempo to something more manageable.

'Hold me,' Anna said.

'That I *can* do,' I said.

I put my hands round her shoulders and drew her towards me. I held her tight and felt her warmth flood my body. She looked into my eyes.

'Isn't this just perfect?' she said. 'Nothing could spoil this moment. And then there's tomorrow to look forward to. It will be the best day of my life. I'm so happy.'

'May you always be so,' I said.

'I will,' she said. 'With you by my side, I will. I love you so much, Johnny. We will stay this happy for ever. Nothing will tear us apart.'

I leant down and kissed her. 'Nothing,' I said.

Not even the bond of friendship.

CHAPTER TWO

As WEDDINGS GO, I doubt there's much difference in the protocol according to whether the ceremony is carried out in a marquee on the manicured lawns of a five-star hotel on a Caribbean island or a dusty damp church in the middle of England. There was a lot of *I do*-ing, tears from the female contingent, fumbling of rings on fingers and the flashes of digital cameras recording every moment for posterity. The bride wore white – pretty much de rigueur, pregnant or not – and the groom broke his usual dress code to wear a lightweight suit in grey with silver pinstripes, a light-blue shirt and dark-blue tie. To say I felt uncomfortable would be a gross understatement. A combination of unfamiliar clothes and the importance of the occasion, I suspected I would have felt more comfortable with a Browning Hi-Power pistol in a shoulder holster, but was wise enough not to mention that fact to Anna or my mother. Bull instinctively knew what I was feeling and grinned at me sadistically.

When it was over, Bull asked us to remain inside for a few minutes and my four mercenary friends slipped away. A little while later there was a cry of, 'You can come out now.' Anna and I, arm in arm, stepped outside. There we saw a guard of honour – Bull and Stan on one side, Red and Pieter on the other, all in camouflage kit with pistols criss-crossed, pointing at the sky. I recognised the weapons as being of no-known make, but I guessed their function. Anna, however, gripped my hand tightly and took a step back. She relaxed when my friends sprayed arcs of water over our heads. Along with the rest of the guests, my mother smiled. I took it as acceptance of my past profession and felt a lump in my throat.

A long table had been set out under sunshades where we would sit, another table was laid with a buffet, including the local delicacy, curried goat. I helped Mother into her seat and whispered in her ear.

'Now tell me what you think of Anna?'

'You're a very lucky man. Anna's beautiful, but I've said that already. She's also a strong woman and that's what you need to keep you in check. You'll be a father soon and you will need to take on new responsibilities. No more gallivanting wherever takes your fancy.' She paused and smiled. 'But don't listen too much to the ramblings of an old woman. Enjoy every day from now into a long and peaceful future.' I may have been wrong, but I think she put a small stress on the word peaceful. 'I know you will do what is right for Anna and your new family. Gus taught you right from wrong, and I guess you will not forget his teachings. We both love you very much, Gus and I. Be happy for us and for yourselves.' She hugged me and kissed me on the cheek. 'Now, away with you and talk to your other guests.'

I circulated for a while and then, as if by some contrivance, the five of us were alone together.

'OK, Stan. Out with it. What happened to your face?' I asked, dreading the answer.

'It's not just my face,' he said. 'I'm all strapped up because I have three broken ribs and my chest is covered in bruises.'

'Who did it to you?' I asked.

'No one you would know.'

'But someone with whom I'd like to get acquainted,' I said.

25

Bull chipped in. 'I'm not sure about the *with whom* bit – kinda too fancy for me – but I echo Johnny's words. Whoever did it, picked on the wrong guy and they will have to pay for that.'

'Tell us more?' Red asked. 'What are you into?'

'Everything was going fine,' Stan said. 'The hotel is running near capacity, the restaurant has a good reputation and you need to book to be sure of a table. Then it started. I had a visit from two thugs. They offered me protection. And when I declined they beat me up – one of them caught me unawares, otherwise I would have put up a better fight.'

'So what's the current situation?' I said.

'I left instructions and some cash with Ho to pay them if they come back while I'm away. Didn't seem to have much choice.'

'Comanche warrior will stand by your side,' said Red. 'We are blood brothers.'

'That goes for me, too,' said Bull.

'If you think I'm being left out of this,' said Pieter, 'then you picked the wrong man.'

All eyes turned to me. I hesitated. The pause spoke volumes.

'I understand,' said Pieter before I could speak. 'You've embarked on a new life. You have Anna and the soon-to-be child to think of. They have to take priority over everything else.'

'Mai Ling is used to me going away,' said Bull. 'And you'll be here to look after her and little Michael. That makes it easier for me to go.'

'I'm sure the four of us can handle everything,' said Red. 'Comanche warrior fight with strength of ten men.'

'You stay,' said Stan. 'Your place is here. Like Pieter said, I understand. Times have changed. Circumstances have changed.' He gave me a weak smile. 'And it's about time we learnt not to rely on you to lead us. Hell, who's going to miss you and your little Uzi? Four Kalashnikovs can handle anything.'

'But the Kalashnikov is notorious for ...'

'We know,' interrupted Bull. 'Notorious for jamming.' He sighed. 'We all have our favourite weapons. We're individuals.'

'But a powerful combination when we're united,' said Pieter.

'Which you won't be this time,' I said. 'And who said you were going to need Kalashnikovs?'

'Pays to be prepared for anything,' said Stan in his usual morose tone.

'We're not going to miss you,' said Red. 'Trust me, paleface.'

How can you trust a man that puts on a Comanche accent when the going gets tough?

Red continued. 'There will still be Stan guarding the back door and handling the logistics. Bull out front where he will frighten the shit out of anyone. Pieter and I will be on the flanks. We can handle a bunch of Polish hoods, no problem.'

'Well,' I said. 'If you're sure.'

'Course we're sure,' said Bull.

'In that case I'll sit this one out.'

'That's settled then,' said Red. 'Now, let's go and try some of the curried goat we've heard so much about.'

We did.

It tasted like ashes in my mouth.

I had a troubled night, tossing and turning, and fitful dreams that exaggerated reality and made them all the more scary. Anna was restless, too, but that wasn't unusual lately. The baby, cocooned in its warm and safe environment, seemed to wake up at night and kick its way till dawn. I gave up on sleep at six, slipped on a pair of swimming shorts and a T-shirt, and made my way to the beach. Bull was there sitting on the jetty, waiting for me.

'Guessed you'd come,' he said. 'Thought you might need an ear.'

'Couldn't sleep,' I said. 'Anyway, what time were you here?'

'Some nights it's good to sleep on the boat, catching the breeze from the sea, watching the dawn break over the horizon.'

'So you spent all night here?'

'You got it,' he said.

'I feel a heel,' I said.

'I imagine that's so. In your place I'd feel the same, but sometimes you have to let someone down in order to look after someone else. It's a hard decision and I don't envy you.'

'So why aren't you going through the same torment. Mai Ling and Michael depend on you, so by rights you should be staying, too?'

'When we took on the Russians in Amsterdam, we all earned a lot of money, thanks to you – a life-changing amount. Red got his ranch, Stan his hotel, Pieter probably spent some of his on women and booze and squandered the rest. For me, some of the money that I got was a saviour – it paid for Michael's heart transplant. I feel I owe the team. There wasn't one of us who was spare. Without us acting as a team, Michael wouldn't be here today. It's a debt I have to repay. But as far as you are concerned, you earned us that money. We owe you, not the other way round. Stay, and don't give it a second thought.'

'But.'

'What kind of mess can we get into that we can't handle? You're the one that trouble follows around like a big black shadow. Hell, we'll probably be safer without you.'

'Gee, thanks.'

'My pleasure.' He gave me a big grin. 'Come on. One last swim to the buoy and run back along the beach before I have to go and get packed. I'd say "for old time's sake", but that kind of seems final.'

'Don't undo all the fine words that were beginning to make me feel better.'

'I suppose sometimes it's better to keep your mouth shut. That's a lesson we both could learn. Especially you. Your wisecracks always seem to fire up the enemy into taking drastic action.'

'Let's have that swim before you think of any more insults.'

I kicked off my shoes and waded into the water. It was crystal clear and I felt invigorated as it flowed over my body. Maybe Bull was right – they'd be fine without me acting like a magnet for trouble. But they had trouble already, if Stan's beaten body was anything to go by. I pushed the unhelpful thought from my mind and started a slow relaxed crawl so that Bull could catch me up – I always believe in a fair contest.

The swim to the buoy took fifteen minutes and then we ran back along the sand. It was a great time of day – although on St Jude there weren't any bad times of day. The sun dried the sea water from us and we gratefully sank down into two of the chairs outside the bar with a couple of bottles of ice-cold beer. Never too early for a bottle of beer, especially if you've worked up a sweat. I saw Anna approaching and immediately felt guilty – maybe she didn't see ice-cold beer at eight in the morning in quite the same way as Bull and I did.

She came and stood behind me and massaged the muscles in my neck.

'You've got an appointment in the bedroom,' she said.

Sometimes it's nice to be dominated.

'Don't let me keep you,' said Bull.

Anna took me by the hand, led me back to our cabin and stood outside the bedroom door.

'You go in and I'll join you in a moment,' she said.

I followed instructions. Stepped through the door and stared. I came back out of the bedroom and looked at her in surprise.

'What's the rucksack doing on the bed?' I asked.

'It was too heavy for me to lift after I had packed it. I hope I haven't forgotten anything.'

'But.'

'Don't try to tell me that you do not want to go.'

'Yes, but.'

'I do not want anyone saying that my man let his friends down. It would be without honour, and I know how important honour is to you. And since I met you it has become important for me, too. I will not be shamed.'

'But you can't run the bar on your own.'

'I won't have to. Gus is going to stay on. He says he needs a break. He can do the heavy work and look after me, if that is what is putting you off going.'

'But he hasn't worked for thirty years. The culture shock could give him a heart attack. And he doesn't know anything about running a bar.'

'Johnny, just how difficult is it?'

'I suppose you're right. When did you cook all this up?'

'Gus and I had a talk last night. After I had spoken to Stan. He didn't say much, but he did not need to. It is all arranged.'

I kissed her, the answer to all my doubts and fears.

'Who said you could come out of the bedroom?'

'But.' I stuttered.

'There's two hours before the boat leaves and I want to make the most of it.'

CHAPTER THREE

It was an arduous journey that seemed to go on forever. It involved the boat to Barbados, two changes of flight and then a local shuttle from Warsaw to Krakow. The shuttle plane held only a dozen people, and we squeezed in alongside some businessmen in dark suits with even darker countenances: maybe they were as happy to be on this tiny plane as we were. In a bid for maximum passenger capacity, the airline had squeezed in four rows of three – a single on the left side and a double on the right – where only three rows should have been allowed. None of us were short, but Bull, with his six-feet-six height, had to contort his body to get into his seat and at the end, stood up to reveal he was bent double. And that wasn't the worst of it. The plane had twin propellers and flew so low that we seemed to fly in constant turbulence, sending my stomach into freefall with every downwards drop and my mind into prayer when we rose again.

As we got off the plane, Pieter said, 'If that flight had gone on any longer, I think I would have converted to Catholicism.'

'I thought of becoming a Buddhist once,' said Stan, deadpan. 'You know the reincarnation thing? But I thought, with my luck, I might come back as myself.'

We all looked at him and he gave a little smile. It was one of the rare moments – not just a joke from Stan, but one that didn't involve dill pickles.

Stan had his car at the airport. It was one of those solid people carriers which had thirty ways to position the seats, and I felt sure that Stan would have experimented with all of them before settling on the current configuration. As we neared our destination, the Carpathians rose above us. Although it was summer, there was snow still on the mountains, such was their height. I could just see a cable car making its way to the top through some wispy clouds.

Stan brought the car to a halt on a ridge and invited us to get out. The view was incredible. Nestling below the Carpathians was a massive lake, its blue waters reflecting the dipping sun. The water was so still that there were perfect reflections of sea birds on the surface of the water.

'That's Lake Cezar,' said Stan. 'Biggest lake in Poland, and Poland has more lakes than anywhere else in the world.

'Comes with the dill pickles, I suppose,' said Pieter.

'Poland is the biggest producer of dill pickles in the world,' said Stan.

'So you've said, many times,' I said.

'Good to have something to be proud of,' Stan said.

'Even if it's only dill pickles,' said Bull.

'Even if it's only dill pickles,' Stan said, nodding. He swept his arm across the vista. 'Well, what do you think?'

'Stunning,' I said. 'Why haven't we heard of this place before? It deserves to be a tourist hotspot.'

Stan nodded. 'We Poles have kept it pretty much to ourselves so far. Where else could you ski in the morning and swim in the crystal clear waters of a lake in the afternoon or vice versa, of course?'

'Of course,' I said.

'Someday the rest of Europe – maybe even the world – will hear of it and it will lose its charm, overrun by fast food joints and American ladies five feet tall in blue.'

I shook my head, trying to make the connection – something to do with Marrakesh, but I couldn't nail it down – but I think I knew what he meant. Seemed that nowadays nowhere was free from the insidious creep of commercialism and cloning by the multi-nationals. I must be getting old, or maybe nostalgia just isn't what it used to be.

'What's that off the shore line?' I asked Stan.

'An island. Bird sanctuary – some sort of rare goose or stork or something. It's off limits now, though. Six months ago, a tourist went to visit the island and had a heart attack. Couldn't get to him in time. The authorities don't want another death so no one's allowed to go there anymore. Health and safety.'

Around the lake ran a promenade along which were dotted a number of buildings that looked like tall Swiss chalets. By their size I took them to be hotels.

'Is one of them yours?' I asked Stan.

'The one flying the five flags,' he replied. 'Isn't she beautiful?'

'Five flags?' I said. 'Isn't that rather overdoing things?'

'One for each of us,' he said. 'After all, it was the money we made in Amsterdam that paid for the hotel.'

'She's beautiful,' said Red.

'I think you've invested wisely,' said Pieter.

'Not if all the profits go on paying protection money,' said Stan.

'They won't,' said Bull. 'We're here now. We can sort this out. Whoever is behind this doesn't know who they're dealing with.'

'Yeah,' said Pieter. 'Think of it. They know as much as we do.'

'Good to start off on level terms,' I said.

'I'd prefer an edge,' said Red.

'We'll get one,' I said. 'We always have in the past.'

'Doesn't it worry you,' Bull said, 'that one day our luck will run out?'

'I try not to think about it.'

'Good plan,' said Bull. 'I feel so much more reassured now.'

We got back in the car and travelled down the winding road from the ridge to the town. Most of the hotels, like Stan's, were five storeys high. They were built of wood, probably pine from my limited knowledge, and had balconies on the rooms fronting onto the lake. The roofs over the top floor windows were triangular, which gave a fairy-tale appearance to the buildings like some castle from a children's picture book.

The hotels were separated from each other by generous gardens. If the place really did catch on in the future, these gardens would be ripe for development. Stan's hotel was to the west of the promenade, the tiled walkway extending to the distance. This was a big resort. I wondered just how full all these hotels were and whether there were seasons when skiing and swimming weren't an option. To me, if the answer was no, then there was big money to be made here.

Stan pulled up in front of the hotel and we piled out of the car and got our luggage. Ho, Stan's Chinese cook and general factotum, must have been watching for us to arrive as she was waiting with the door open. She kissed each of us on the cheek and ushered us inside. Pieter had a stupid grin on his face and I knew what was coming. Please don't say it, I thought. My wish was not to be granted.

'Hi, Ho,' he said, laughing fit to burst.

'Joke is even better second time I hear it, honourable Pieter,' she said, managing to keep her emotions in check.

'Good to see you again,' said Red, her former employer before Stan had poached her from him.

Ho gave him a big hug and smiled broadly. We all towered

over her and she looked so small and vulnerable, but we knew she could pack a kung fu punch when necessary. What she lacked in height she made up with a classic Chinese bone structure that made her beautiful. She came from the south of China and had a westernised face rather than the Mongolian flat features of those who came from the north. She was wearing a smart uniform of blue jacket and skirt with a white blouse open at the collar and black flat shoes. She looked the model of efficiency. But when you worked with Stan, nothing else would do.

'Come,' she said to all of us. 'I will get you keys to your rooms. Settle selves in and refresh from journey.'

She led us to a reception desk in some sort of dark wood – trees are not one of my specialist subjects – with a large ledger lying on top. She consulted the ledger and turned round to pick keys from a set of cubby holes and handed them to us.

'I will make coffee,' she said. 'How long will you need?'

'Give us fifteen minutes,' I said, anxious to get the lay of the land and see what defences could be mounted if the worse came to the worst and we were under threat.

Ho nodded and walked across the reception area and through a door marked 'Private'. It was our cue to climb the stairs and go to our rooms.

'I asked Ho to give you the best rooms,' Stan said. 'I hope you like them. If there is anything you need, just let me know. I will check on the arrangements for dinner and join you for coffee.'

Pieter and Red had rooms on the second floor and Bull and I next to each other on the top. I went inside, put my luggage on the bed and walked to the floor-to-ceiling glass doors. Don't rent this out to anyone with vertigo, I thought. The room was at the front of the building and looked out over the lake. I opened the doors to the balcony and stood there in awe. The view was magnificent. The lake was an iridescent blue, and the setting sun picked out some small boats with white sails that were making their way to the shore. A few stratus clouds ran in straight horizontal lines across the red of the sky. It was like a posed picture by a watercolour artist. This place could be heaven.

'Some view,' said Bull from the balcony next to mine.

'This is the sort of place worth fighting for,' I said.

'Which no doubt we'll be doing,' he replied.

'It might not come to that.'

'You used that *might* word again. Something bad always happens when you use the *might* word.'

'There's got to be a first time.'

Bull gave a grunt, which I took to mean a sardonic reply.

'Hasn't there?' I said.

He grunted again.

'Maybe you're right,' I said. 'The law of averages doesn't seem to apply to us.'

'No laws apply to us. We make our own rules and follow our own code. That's what makes us strong.'

'Deep stuff,' I said.

'Man's got a right to be a philosopher sometimes.'

'Reckon so.'

'What was it Martin Luther King once said?' he asked.

'"If a man hasn't found something worth dying for, he isn't fit to live."'

He nodded his head and there was silence between us for a while.

'Hell,' Bull said finally, 'I need a drink.'

'Now you're talking my language.'

I showered to wash away the dust of the journey, put on a

clean black T-shirt and a pair of khaki chinos and went downstairs. I was the first to arrive in the sitting room so had my pick of the seats. It was a large room with wooden – of course – tables and wingback easy chairs with seats padded in a dark floral print. I lowered myself into one of the chairs: out of habit, one with my back to the wall and a view of the door. The chair was soft and cosy, and I gave a little sigh as I rested limbs that had spent too long cramped up by sitting down that day. I stretched my legs and relaxed.

One by one the others joined me. We rearranged some of the chairs so that we could sit in a close circle. The others had changed, too, and we looked smart but casual as if we didn't have a care in the world.

Ho arrived with a silver tray with a coffee pot, five white mugs, sugar, cream, a bottle of vodka with ice surrounding it and five shot glasses. Stan, the perfect host, poured the coffee and the vodka and placed each on the table in the middle of our group. We downed the vodka – it had a kick like a bad-tempered mule – and he refilled the glasses nonetheless.

'That's better,' Pieter said. 'I'm beginning to feel human again.'

'Must be a first for you,' Red said with a laugh.

Stan wasn't in a laughing mood. 'Ho, tell everybody what happened while I was away.'

'Two men come. Big men. Look like boxers. Broken noses.'

'Couldn't have been very good boxers,' said Bull. 'Not if their faces were like that.'

'If it's the same two that assaulted me,' Stan said, 'then they couldn't have been that bad either. But, go on, Ho.'

'I do as you say, Stan. I give them the money. They didn't trust me. Counted it very slowly like it was a hard task.'

'Sounds like we outgun them in the brains department,' I said.

37

'I'll think of that,' said Bull, 'when I'm picking bullets out of my chest.'

Ho continued. 'They say they come back next week on same day – Sunday afternoon when we big money from weekend. That if we don't want trouble we pay. He say I have pretty face and would want to keep it that way.'

'Was this conversation in English?' I asked. I doubted whether Ho had managed to pick up much Polish in the three months or so she had been there.

She nodded.

'English is spoken widely in Poland,' said Stan. 'We teach it in school as a second language. It's also the language of business. Lots of multi-nationals have offices here. Warsaw mostly, but a few in the industrial areas like Kielce.'

'OK,' I said. 'That means that we can split up easily – we won't need Stan to translate all the time.'

'Don't worry me,' said Bull. 'I can grunt in Polish pretty good.'

'What are our assets?' I asked Stan.

'Gun laws in Poland are liberal since they were reformed in 2011. As long as you have a valid reason, like hunting, don't have a criminal record and aren't a hazard, then ownership is allowed.'

'One out of three isn't bad,' Bull said.

'I've arranged for us to go to a gun club,' Stan said. 'We can buy guns there and have a practice at the same time. The only downside is that we'll have to stick to hand guns and hunting rifles. We couldn't make a convincing case that we go hunting with Kalashnikovs.'

'Hardly fair on the squirrels,' said Red. 'Comanche warrior not stoop that low.' He paused. 'How about sawn-off shotguns?'

Stan considered this for a moment. 'They could be OK.'

'That's me smiling,' Red said.

'Make that a shotgun for each of us,' I said.

'A bit crude,' Bull said, 'but I'm happy to go along with that, providing you all keep silent about it. Got a reputation to uphold.'

Pieter opened his mouth to speak and thought better of it.

'And you say,' I said to Ho, 'that they are coming back on Sunday?'

She nodded.

'That gives us three days to come up with a plan,' I said.

'No,' said Bull. 'It gives us three days to come up with a plan that doesn't involve people shooting at us.'

'Picky, picky,' I said.

Ho looked at Stan and he nodded his head. She did a little bow. 'I go finish preparations for dinner,' she said. 'Stan has taught me how to cook traditional Polish food.'

I couldn't wait. One hundred and one things to do with pickled cucumbers.

She walked from the room and we helped ourselves to more coffee and vodka, hoping that the effects of one would counterbalance those of the other.

'Tomorrow,' I said to Stan, 'you give us a guided tour of the hotel so that we can see the layout and consider firing positions – although I suspect you have already got those mapped out – and then take in the area around the lake. Maybe even a ride on the cable car to the top of the mountain, see it in all its glory.'

Stan looked at his watch. 'We can eat, if you're ready.'

'Boy, am I ready,' said Red. 'I could eat a horse.'

'Don't commit yourself,' I said. 'We don't know the local customs yet.'

'Do you think we are uncivilized?' Stan said, sounding affronted. 'We wouldn't eat horse. Well, not on a Thursday.'

We smiled as one and rose from our seats. Followed him

into the dining room. The Swiss chalet style continued. There were ten square tables seating four people and two that were rectangular and seated six. The tables were a dark wood with pink tablecloths set to leave four exposed triangles at the corners of the table. On each table was a small lamp with a bulb that mimicked a candle, giving a soft warm glow. It was the kind of place you could relax in, feel comfortable. If the food matched the ambiance, then Stan was on a winner.

He led us to a table for four and explained that he had to help out with waiting and that he hoped we would enjoy our traditional Polish meal.

The first dish to arrive, we were reliably informed by Stan, was *barszcz czerwony*, a red beetroot soup with cream and dumplings. It was accompanied by more vodka, neat. The soup was better than the colour suggested, but was very filling. I'd never be able to pronounce the name, but I never intended to order it again so that worked out fine. I was tempted to leave some of the dumplings, but didn't want to offend Stan. Next came *pierogi*, potato cakes with a mixture of cold meats and sausages: I could sense a theme going on and it was gluttony. Stan had brought Polish beers to go with the potato cakes: the beers were much lighter than we were used to, but helped to wash down the starchy potatoes. The main course, *bigos*, was a 'hunter's stew', a kind of sauerkraut dish laced with pork, game, more sausage and bacon. It was accompanied by a deep dish containing mixed vegetables and another of boiled potatoes. This time the complementary drink that Stan had selected was Hungarian red wine – presumably the Poles didn't produce their own, otherwise we'd have been drinking that – and matched the dish well. By this stage we were all struggling and dreading what was to come as dessert. It was éclairs filled with cream and covered in rich dark chocolate. I doubted whether I'd ever be able to move again.

We leaned back in our chairs and heaved a big sigh. Another mouthful and we would have exploded. Stan came across and looked at us expectantly.

'Well?' he said. 'How was it?'

'It was good,' I said, caught in Morton's Fork – I had to praise it, but not so much that he would serve the same meal tomorrow. 'But how do you keep yourself in shape eating this sort of food?'

'I don't eat this stuff,' he said. 'I'd be as fat as a pig if I did. I usually just have a steak and a salad.'

Always eat what the host has. I should have checked that before.

'I need to walk this off,' said Bull.

There were nods around the table.

'Give me ten minutes,' said Stan, 'and I'll take you to the main square. I'll send some coffee over.'

When he was gone, we resumed our slumped states and emitted the occasional groan.

'At least we know what to have tomorrow,' said Pieter.

'If we kept on eating this food,' said Red, 'then we'd be a walkover for whoever is the opposition.'

'We know what to do to get them to surrender, though,' I said. 'Feed them.'

'That's sadistic,' Bull said. 'I wouldn't sink that low. Well, only on a bad day like when you keep using the *might* word. Or the *maybe* one, that always winds me up, too.'

'Why are the words *short* and *fuse* entering my head?' I said.

'Don't ask me,' Bull said. 'I can't be responsible for your mind, I have enough trouble being responsible for Pieter's body.'

'What do you mean by that?' said Pieter.

'I think he means,' I said, 'no getting us into fights because

41

of women. And that is doubly so for Ho. Stan obviously has a thing for her so don't give him cause for concern.'

'What do you take me for?' said Pieter. 'I'm old enough to be her father.'

'You could even *be* her father the way you put yourself about in the past,' Red said.

'Don't you start, too,' said Pieter. 'I've got my own moral code, although it might not be obvious at first sight.' Bull raised his eyebrows at this. 'I'm not a cradle snatcher. And anyway, I get enough sex on my safaris, so I don't need any more from girls as young as Ho.'

'Good to know,' I said. 'And thanks for sharing that.'

Stan walked into the room and immediately sensed an atmosphere – it's unlike us to go quiet all of a sudden.

'What's going on?' he asked.

'Nothing,' I said. 'Just recovering from the sumptuous feast. Giving our mouths a rest.'

He looked at me quizzically and shrugged.

'Come on, Stan,' Pieter said. 'Let's lead the way.'

We went out the front of the hotel and turned left, heading along the promenade. From the first hotel we passed, there was the sound of raised voices. Although my knowledge of Polish was less than zero, I could tell from the tone of the voices that an argument was going on. Not good for the public image of the hotel, broadcasting your disagreements in public.

We headed past and carried on walking. It was a balmy night and was warm enough for us not to need jackets. A slight breeze was blowing over the lake and the moon glinted off the surface. Pretty close to idyllic. Would have been so if the comparison wasn't against St Jude.

After five minutes of passing hotels similar to Stan's, we came to an open plaza. There was a variety of bars and restaurants and some shops selling designer gear that only rich Poles could afford – maybe only rich Poles came here. We strolled past and continued along the promenade. After only a couple of minutes, we could see the cable car. It was an acrophobic's nightmare. Not only did the cable car run steeply upwards to the top of the nearest mountain, but it was completely constructed of some thick, clear plastic material – Plexiglas, probably. So anyone standing inside only had to look down to see the sheer drop below. I had no fear of heights, but I doubted whether even I would look down much. Too many ways to die without being prompted on another one. I imagine if Stan were to take a trip in the cable car he would bring along a length of rope, a flask of hot coffee and another of brandy, the Polish equivalent of Kendal Mint Cake and a couple of blankets to cover all eventualities.

After another five minutes of passing more hotels, we turned back and headed for the plaza. It was still buzzing – couples, mostly, enjoying a drink and a liqueur before turning in for the night. There were a few families, too, children happy to run around the square free of parental control apart from a roving watchful eye. We found a table big enough for all five of us and ordered coffee and, taking our lives in our hands, Polish brandy. It had a certain fire that made you feel that you could endure anything from that moment on.

'How are your ribs, Stan?' I asked once I had recovered my voice.

'They hurt only when I laugh,' he said.

'So no pain then,' said Bull.

Stan grinned and then winced.

'You're a lucky man, Stan,' I said. 'This is a great place to live, surrounded by people having a good time. It's got a great ambiance.'

Bull mouthed *ambiance*, shook his head and suppressed a grin.

'I know what you mean,' said Pieter. 'You get a feel for a place when you first experience it. It's the same for my clients on safari. They almost become different people in their new surroundings. They relax and let their natural emotions take over.'

'Comanches are big on the feel of somewhere and the spirits that dwell there. They believe that the environment contains a soul and it can be good or bad. This place has a good soul.'

'But—' said Stan.

'You don't have to say anything,' I said. 'You don't have to worry. We'll get this little problem sorted out by the end of the week and we can all return to normal after that.'

I was about to venture another sip of brandy when Pieter, who has the sharpest eyes of all of us, stood up and looked into the distance.

'What's up?' I asked.

'Over there,' he said. 'That glow. It looks like a fire. Pretty big one, too.'

'Oh, God!' Stan said, leaping to his feet. 'My hotel!'

We ran as one, Bull trying to keep up as best as his hamstrung leg would allow. The glow got bigger, an orange flare flowing up to the sky like a volcanic eruption, flames silhouetted against the black of the night sky. My mind filled with dread. Was Stan going to lose everything?

As we got within a hundred yards, the source of the fire was clear. It wasn't Stan's hotel, it was the one next to it, the one where I had heard the altercation as we passed.

The hotel was burning quickly, all that wood in the fabric of the building and the fixtures and fittings feeding the flames. There was a small crowd outside, some, judging by their nightclothes, who looked like people who had escaped from the fury inside, others just onlookers fascinated by the

ONE BULLET TOO MANY

drama that was unfolding. We came to a stop outside and looked up. Against the licking of the flames, I could see a figure on the top floor. Standing on the balcony was a woman in a nightdress which was blowing in the breeze. She was screaming in terror, not able to go inside and no alternative available. Soon, very soon, the fire would reach her.

'Get a duvet,' I said to Stan. 'The biggest and thickest you can find. And be as quick as you can. There isn't much time.'

'What are you thinking?' Red asked.

'She's no option. She's got to jump. We'll spread the duvet, take one corner each, and get her to jump into it.'

'Hell of a jump,' Red said. 'Must be forty feet up to that top floor balcony. I wouldn't like to do it.'

'Jump or fry,' I said. 'No other choice.'

Bull caught us up just as Stan arrived back with a thick double duvet. I explained the plan. Four of us took a corner each and I told Bull to be ready to catch the woman if she bounced off.

'Stan, tell her jump,' I said.

He shouted up in Polish and the woman looked down. Then she just stood there.

'She's frozen,' Bull said.

We'd seen it before in combat situations. A man under threat who freezes, brain shut down by the consequences before him, muscles refusing to act, rooted to the spot.

'Someone's going to have to go up,' Bull said. 'Persuade her to jump or, failing that, resort to throwing her off.'

There was a drainpipe running down the right side of the balcony. It would be possible to climb up that, but it wouldn't be easy. Thank God it wasn't raining and the drainpipe slippery.

'I'm too heavy,' Bull said. 'Might not take my weight.'

All eyes were on me.

'Hell,' I said. 'Red, you make a back for me. Bull, get close to Red. I'm going to climb on his back and then on your shoulders. It'll give me a start and save ten feet or so.'

I hopped on Red's back, up on to Bull's shoulders, reached up as far as I could and grasped the drainpipe. Hauled myself up. As I climbed, I could hear her screams get louder and more frantic. Wouldn't be long before the fire reached the wood of the balcony. How long would it hold when that happened? I brushed the unhelpful thought aside and concentrated on climbing. My technique was the same as if climbing a rope. I crossed my feet around the drainpipe and used them as an anchor while pulling up with my hands. It was slow going.

Halfway up, I was aware of some give in the drainpipe. It was coming away from its fixtures. As I climbed higher, the movement became more noticeable as my weight shifted the centre of gravity around the bolts and pulled the pipe further away from the wall. I was within a few feet when it gave way. As it swung out into thin air, I managed to grab hold of the bottom of the balcony and hung there for a moment, suspended above the pavement where hopefully the duvet was well-positioned and would catch me if I fell. I reached up with my left arm and got some purchase on the balcony, hauled myself up a few feet and then swung my right arm up and caught the top of the railing. I heaved, swung my right leg up and placed it on the balcony floor. I pulled myself over the railings and stood beside the woman. She was still transfixed. The heat was almost unbearable. I didn't know how much time we had left, but it couldn't be long now.

'Jump!' I shouted at her. 'You have to jump.'

She looked behind her at the flames and stared back at me.

'Jump!' I shouted again, but I wasn't getting through to her. Her senses had shut down.

I slapped her face and she stared at me again, still

unseeing. I pushed her to the edge of the balcony. The glass in the doors shattered and flames spurted out. I lifted her up and threw her over the balcony. Watched her drop into the duvet. My turn next. With flames licking around my body, I climbed over the railings, looked down to see the duvet ready and jumped. It bounced and I rose a few feet into the air before landing safely. I let out a sigh. I could do with a shot of that Polish brandy right now.

Bull slapped me on the back and smiled. 'Left that a bit late, didn't you?'

'I was looking for a marshmallow to toast.'

Stan was marshalling the people from the burning hotel and leading them inside his place. In the distance I could hear the sound of a siren. I wondered how much of the building they could save when they finally arrived. My guess was not much. It was already starting to fall in on itself as the lower floors collapsed. It was then that I noticed it. I was looking at the pavement underneath the window at the front of the hotel. It was a bottle with a blackened rag inside – Molotov cocktail that hadn't burned away. Bull noticed it, too. He turned to me and shook his head.

'It's started, hasn't it?' he asked.

'Reckon so,' I said.

'No *mights*? No *maybes*?'

'No, it's started,' I said. 'Now we have to finish it.'

CHAPTER FOUR

'This is a crap place to defend,' Red said.

'Suddenly I can understand Comanche,' I said.

We were sitting in the lounge of Stan's hotel, surrounded by refugees from the burnt-out hotel next door. They were wrapped in blankets and duvets and looked stunned, as if they couldn't believe what had happened. The proprietor was slumped forwards in an armchair with his head in his hands. The woman who we had rescued from the balcony was gripping the life-saving duvet like a child who thought she might lose her comfort blanket. Ho had made pots of coffee, tea and hot chocolate and given everyone a shot glass of the lethal Polish brandy. Silence reigned, so we kept our voices low as if in a library run by Conan the Librarian.

Stan was on the phone to the other hotels, trying to find rooms for the refugees. We four had volunteered to double up, thereby freeing up two rooms, one for the proprietor, the other for the balcony woman.

The four of us sipped brandy and drank sugary black coffees, knowing that sleep was going to be a luxury we couldn't afford tonight.

'I know what Red means,' said Pieter. 'The hotel is too close to the action, too many people passing by and getting in our lines of fire.'

'We could create some temporary barricades,' said Red.

'Wheel them out when the trouble starts to keep the innocent away.'

'And who is going to man them?' I said. 'If it's two of us, we've split our forces – never a good idea.'

'Don't you think,' Bull said, 'we should talk to the owner of the hotel before we get carried away? For all we know, it could be some Polish equivalent of a blood feud and nothing to do with Stan and the protection racket.'

'Do you really believe that?' I asked.

'No,' he said. 'Too much of a coincidence. But we should talk to the owner anyway. Might find out something useful.'

'Agreed,' I said.

I poured the shot glass of brandy into my coffee and went over to join the unlucky owner. He was still wearing his work clothes: a dark blue suit, white shirt and blue tie. Against the white background of the shirt there were flecks of black soot from the fire. He brushed at them ineffectually, merely spreading the black across a wider area. I held out my hand and introduced myself. He gripped my hand and I could feel the shakes going through his body. I caught Ho's eye and gestured at the man's shot glass. She brought over the bottle and I told her to leave it. I refilled his glass, he drank it down, gave a shiver and I refilled the glass again. The brandy got him talking.

'Tomas,' he said. 'Pleased to meet you. I saw what you did to rescue the lady on the top floor. Took some courage.'

'Just a head for heights,' I said. 'Nothing fancy. Easier to climb a drainpipe than a rope – the rope's always moving.'

'Like the drainpipe,' he said.

'You can't cover every angle. Although that's our aim.'

'I wish I'd done that.'

'Hindsight's a rare gift,' I said. 'Tell me what happened tonight, or what you think happened.'

'It all started a couple of weeks ago. Two men came and told me I needed protection, and that I had to pay for it. They said a lot of things could happen to a hotel if it wasn't protected. And to the guests, too.' He looked across at me, his eyes moist. 'They also made it plain that I shouldn't go to the police. That would only make matters worse.'

'So you paid them?'

'I could just about afford the first payment. We've been refurbishing the rooms, so some were empty and not earning any money, and the work took pretty much all of our spare money. So I paid them and hoped they wouldn't be coming back.'

'But they did.'

'That's when things got frightening. I'm not a brave man, and I'm not a coward either, but I was scared. I was caught in a trap. I couldn't pay them the next time. All our cash had gone. I had a loan from the bank for the refurbishment, but they wouldn't advance any more. I was in a fix.'

'So what did you do then? They obviously didn't beat you up – you've got no outward signs of injuries. Why didn't they use any rough stuff on you?'

'They were too clever for that. They hit me where I was weakest. They gave my wife a beating. Hit her so hard they broke her arm. They made it clear it would be worse next time. For her and for me. They gave me two days to raise the money.'

'Which, I presume from the consequences, you couldn't.'

'I didn't think they'd do anything like this. I thought they would just give me a beating – I'd sent my wife to stay with her sister, so she was safe. They didn't believe I couldn't pay. Thought I was holding out on them.'

'So that was what the raised voices were about?'

'They said they couldn't let me off. That it was bad for

business. They were going to have to make an example of me.'

'Pretty effective example, too. Who's going to want to cross them now?'

'Where do I go from here?' he said, staring at the shot glass. 'I've lost my home, my business, my whole life. What do I do now?'

'Have another brandy. Get some sleep and in the morning contact your insurers. You'll find a way to rebuild what you had.'

'But what's the point? They'll keep coming back for more money. I can't pay them and survive. I might as well just give in. It's hopeless.'

'They won't be coming back. We're going to sort out this mess. Drive them out of town.'

His gaze moved from the glass to look me in the eye. He shuddered.

'You will, too, won't you?' he said. 'I can tell by your eyes. I've seen eyes like that before in the army. They're killing eyes.' He smiled. 'Whoever is behind this is in for one hell of a shock. Good luck, mister. I'll be rooting for you.'

I refilled his shot glass and stood up. A voice called to me.

'Young man.' It was the woman from the balcony. 'Could you come here?'

I walked across the room to where she was sitting, enveloped in the duvet. There was a mug of hot chocolate on the table in front of her. She picked it up with both hands like it was gold dust and took a sip. She breathed a sigh and looked up at me.

'Come sit with me. Indulge an old woman for a while.'

I sat down in an armchair opposite her and looked her over. From the bottom of the folds of the duvet, I could see the hem of a pink cotton nightdress and matching slippers with white bobbles. I guessed she was around sixty from her grey hair, the lines around her eyes and the brown spots on her hands. She had the hard features of a classical Roman lady – high forehead, aquiline nose. This was a plain lady now and would have been so in her distant youth. Yet there was something about her eyes that promised a warmth, if you could get close enough.

'You will have to forgive me,' she said. 'Most unusual for me. I must look a mess.'

'Style tip number one. Always brush your hair before jumping off a balcony.'

'If you remember correctly, I didn't exactly jump,' she said. 'But I'm grateful for what you did. I hate to think what might have happened if you hadn't been around.'

'All part of the service. I'm Johnny Silver. You can call me Johnny.'

'Oh, no, Mr Silver. I don't think that would be appropriate. We have only just met.'

'And already I've seen you in a nightdress. Must count for something.'

'My name is Mrs Obywotel. The nearest English translation of that is Freeman. So you may call me Mrs Freeman.'

We shook hands. Hers was cold as if the blood wasn't circulating properly.

'How are you feeling, Mrs Freeman? You've had quite a night.'

'A little shaky, but that will pass soon. A little foolish, too.'

'And that will pass soon, too,' I said.

'I feel a wreck. Strange how not looking one's best can have a demoralizing influence on one.'

'Your English is very good.'

'I should hope so, seeing that I *am* English and that I teach English for a living.'

'Then I will watch my grammar – or is that *shall*?'

'Have breakfast with me tomorrow, Mr Silver. Meet me at eight, on the dot mind – I hate unpunctuality. Hopefully, I will be back to my best and have regained my composure. I have so many questions for you, but the arms of Morpheus wait to enwrap me.'

'It will be my pleasure, Mrs Freeman. But I have many questions for you, too.'

'I warn you. Old people love to talk. You will not get off lightly. Goodnight, Mr Silver.'

I rejoined our group. Red was taking another shot of brandy.

'You know,' he said, 'this brandy kinda creeps up on you.'

'Like a stalker,' said Pieter.

'With malicious intent,' added Bull.

Stan came to join us. He heaved a sigh. Job well done, I guessed. He placed a large piece of paper on the table in front of him. Looking closely, I could see that it was a spreadsheet: names of hotels constituted the columns and a list of people formed the rows. He had put ticks in all the columns and made some into a cross by adding a diagonal line.

'Plan go well?' I asked

He nodded. 'Everyone has a bed for the night.'

'And what are the crosses?'

'Those who we had to get clothes for. Can't have them wandering around in their nightclothes tomorrow.'

'Ah, tomorrow,' I said. 'We're going to need your meticulous planning then. Hell of a lot to do. Events tonight mean we could well have less time than we thought.'

'I'll take first watch,' said Bull.

'But we don't have any weapons,' said Pieter. 'What are you going to do if trouble starts?'

'Show them my moves – jiu jitsu, karate and kendo.'

'Which one is kendo?' said Red.

'The one with the stick,' said Bull.

'And what are you going to do for a stick?' Pieter asked.

'I like to improvise.'

'So it's kendo without the stick?' I said.

'You got it,' Bull said to me. 'Anyway, what's your plan?'

'I thought I would shout Boo,' I said.

'Simple but effective,' said Pieter.

'A character study in three words,' said Bull.

CHAPTER FIVE

WE MET AT seven o'clock for breakfast. I wanted a good hour of planning strategy and tactics before being both polite and curious and joining Mrs Freeman. Ho hadn't bothered to ask us what we each wanted, but had just served everything on a plate. There were fried eggs, crispy bacon – pandering to Red's Texan tastes, I assumed – two strong meaty sausages which Pieter said reminded him of wildebeest and the rest of us had to take his word, sauté potatoes, tomatoes and mushrooms. If I carried on eating like this, I would need a month in a gym to get back into shape.

We were the only ones in the dining room at that time, the other guests, after the excitement of the night before, opting for a lie in. Or maybe they all had hangovers from the Polish brandy. Stan's bruises were receding and he was able to eat relatively normally, which for him meant long-term planning so as to ensure that he had one piece of everything on his fork for his last bite. After he had successfully finished his breakfast, he took a pad and pen and set them on the table next to his right hand.

'Shall we start with defence or attack?' he asked.

'Defence,' I said. 'Last night showed just how vulnerable these hotels are. All that wood makes them a tinder box. We have to combat the use of Molotov cocktails first and foremost.'

'Are fire extinguishers too obvious to mention?' asked Pieter.

'Got them on the list,' said Stan. 'Fire blankets, too. Swamp the hotel with them so wherever you are there's something nearby.'

'What about fixing shutters on all the windows?' Red said.

Stan thought for a moment. 'Wouldn't work if they were fixed outside – the attackers could simply open them – and if fixed inside then the petrol could run down and a fire would still break out.'

'Mosquitoes,' Pieter said.

'What the hell have mosquitoes got to do with it?' asked Bull.

'In South Africa, if you can't afford air conditioning, you need to leave the windows open to let the breeze through and the air to circulate, but if you do that the mosquitoes get in. So they fix a very fine mesh to the windows – big enough to let air in, but small enough so that the mosquitoes can't get through. If we put the fine mesh over the windows, anything thrown would bounce off. OK, you might have a fire start outside, but that's more manageable.'

'Genius,' Stan said, making a note on his pad. 'The balconies might represent a problem, but if we have enough fire extinguishers, any fires that start there can quickly be put out.'

'What's to the rear of the hotel?' I asked. We still had to do our reconnaissance in daylight, but I wanted as much information as possible now, since time could well be short.

'A flat terrace and then a slight incline,' Stan said, 'before getting steeper the closer you get to the top of the Carpathians.'

'So, accessible,' I said.

'Too much so,' said Stan. 'We'd need to guard the rear as

well as the front of the hotel.'

'What about tripwires?' said Red. 'Some network of wires that would alert us to anyone moving around out there? Be a waste of manpower to have someone stationed at the back all the time.'

'But how do we hear that someone has passed through the tripwires?' I asked.

'Baby alarm,' said Bull. 'Mai Ling and I used one when Michael was small. We simply put bells connected to the trip wires. Place a baby alarm outside and the receiver on reception. That's the central point downstairs. If we turn one up to maximum sensitivity, we'd hear it most anywhere downstairs.'

'I'm still worried about attack from the front where there would be too many innocent passers-by,' I said. 'We've talked about barricades, I can't see anything better than that – still takes two of us to man them. Weakens us a hell of a lot.'

'Ho could help out,' Stan said. 'She can handle herself with her kung fu or whatever it is.'

'But can she handle a gun?' Pieter asked.

'Wasn't on my job specification when I was recruiting a cook,' said Stan. 'But we could give her some practice. The gun club has a shooting range. She can have some sessions there. Enough so she could defend herself at close range at least.'

'I like this,' I said. 'It's beginning to all come together.'

'With no *mights* or *maybes*,' said Bull.

'Don't worry,' I said. 'I expect I can come up with a few of those.'

'Just when it was going so well,' said Bull, shaking his head.

'Firing positions,' I said. 'Pieter, can you handle those?'

'Be glad to,' he replied.

'Red, I want Stan to give you a tour of the area and for you to get used to his car. We may well need to use your driving skills.'

Although, *skills* was not quite the right word. *Tendencies* might have fitted better. Just short of *recklessness* even. But he drove fast and that could come in useful.

'He's not driving my car,' Stan said, panic just under control. 'I'll hire another.'

'Something inconspicuous,' I said. I had a role in mind for Red. 'We seem to have pretty much covered defence. Let's move on to attack.'

'First thing we got to do,' said Bull, 'is get some weapons. I feel naked in this situation without a gun, and preferably an assault rifle, too.'

I looked at Stan's notepad. Two columns headed Attack and Defence. He started writing under "Attack". Gun club in capital letters.

'We can pick up some handguns at the gun club. Assault rifles, as I said before, might be a problem.'

'Don't you start using the *might* word, too,' said Bull. 'I've enough trouble with Johnny.'

'Doubt whether we could get an Uzi for you, Johnny,' Stan said. 'Kalashnikovs produced around here – too plentiful, too cheap for anything else to be considered. I'll have to try to get those on the black market, maybe go to Krakow.'

'How about a sniper rifle?' I said.

'How about a shotgun?' added Red.

'Sniper rifle used for hunting, shotgun, too. Shouldn't have too much trouble there. Might not be the Dragunov, though.'

'What is this? Deprive Johnny of His Favourite Weapons Week?'

'Not much call for Uzis or Dragunovs around here. Not since we got civilized at any rate.'

'Depends on your definition of civilization,' I said. 'I

wouldn't call what happened last night civilized.'

'Takes only one evil man,' Bull said, 'to make a country uncivilized.'

'And five to put it right again,' I said. 'At least that's what I'm hoping.'

'As long as they have guns,' Pieter said.

'Gun club in an hour,' Stan said. 'Let's get tooled up. Meanwhile, I'll arrange a car for Red.'

'Something with some guts,' said Red.

'Don't worry. I have something in mind.' Stan stood up from the table. 'I'll send over some more coffee,' he said. 'Best be at maximum alert from now on.'

There were nods around the table. As Stan reached the door, he paused, stepped aside and opened it wide for Mrs Freeman. She was wearing black trousers and a black loose-fit top which I guessed was Ho's. It was a good fit for a makeshift outfit, a little short in the leg perhaps but showed off the black pumps to perfection. She would need to go on a shopping trip after breakfast – bound to be some female necessities to buy as well as new clothes. I wondered what else she'd lost in the fire – passport, money, jewellery – and how easy it would be to replace. Maybe some had survived the inferno. We'd soon find out when we went outside.

I waited till she had selected a table and settled down, and then went over to her. Ho must have found her some make-up, too, because she looked bright and fresh and ready to face life's tribulations.

I put my hand on the back of a chair and said, 'With your permission?'

'Do sit down,' she said. 'And how are we this morning?'

'I'm fine. How about you?'

'I'm fine, too. Thank you for enquiring.'

'I've been trying to think up an opening line,' I said, 'but can't come up with anything better than "What's a nice girl like you doing in a joint like this?"'

'If you're going to call me a girl, I'll overlook the cliché.'

'How did you sleep?' I asked.

'Surprisingly well. I feel ready to face what I guess will be a difficult day. I am hoping that the hotel safe will have survived the fire – my money and passport were in there.'

'Good chance,' I said.

'You must bear with me for a moment while I get some food from the buffet – I am absolutely ravenous. I suspect it's all the excitement. I'm not used to it.'

'Few people are,' I said. 'Go ahead and get something to eat. I've got a lot of coffee to drink and only a hour to do it in.'

She rose from the table and moved across to where Ho had laid out a selection of fruit and cereals and a variety of cold meat and cheeses. She scanned it all for a while and then put some muesli in a bowl and topped it with fruit and yoghurt. She then loaded up a plate with the meats and cheese. She walked back with the smile of someone who was already savouring the food. I rose from my chair until she had arrived back to the table and had taken her seat. Stan followed her back and she ordered tea. I sipped my coffee and let her eat for a while before asking any questions.

'How long have you been in Poland?' I asked.

'Must be ten years now – I almost qualify as a native. I met my husband in London – he was a Pole working for the embassy. It was a whirlwind romance and a great surprise. I had almost resigned myself to the lifetime role of spinster. We were so much in love. It was a marvellous time.'

She became quiet for a moment, simply staring at her food.

But destined not to last, I guessed.

'He was posted back to Poland and we lived in an apartment in Warsaw. I loved Warsaw so much, so cosmopolitan, such a feeling for the arts – opera, ballet, music. You must go there.' She poured herself some tea and looked disdainfully at the weak liquid that entered her cup. She added a little milk and took an experimental sip. She unsuccessfully fought back a wince. 'No one makes tea like the British,' she said. 'It's one of the few things I miss from England.'

'The coffee's better,' I said. 'Thick and black, rich in flavour.'

'I know what to order next time.'

'You're staying?'

'Can't go back to a burnt-out shell. Stanislav says I can stay as long as I like.'

I let her attack the muesli for a while and contented myself to sipping coffee.

'When did you start to teach?' I asked.

'When I first got to Poland, I occupied myself with exploring Warsaw and visiting galleries and exhibitions – I had so much time on my hands. But, after a while, I needed something more stimulating to occupy myself. My Polish had become very good by that stage, so I did some tutoring for the children of civil servants and those who wanted their offspring to have a career with the multi-nationals. They have a flair for language, the Poles – it must be all the past adaptations they had to make to those who conquered the country. Teaching was both pleasurable and immensely enjoyable. I had everything – a doting husband, all the creature comforts you could wish for and an occupation that I loved. Yes, some of the children were, shall we say, challenging, but it was terribly rewarding when I eventually got through to them.'

We were getting close to the *but* now. I refilled her teacup to give her time to gather her thoughts and find the words to fit. She pushed the empty muesli bowl aside and cut a piece of cheese. She popped it in her mouth and smiled.

'The Poles make good cheese,' she said. 'You should try some.'

'No, thanks,' I said. 'I'm not going to eat for a week. Maybe longer.'

She placed a small slice of smoked ham on a piece of bread and then sat there staring at it.

'It's good to talk,' I said. 'Sometimes better with a stranger, too.'

'Well,' she said, 'you've probably guessed what is coming. It's a story without a happy ending. My husband had a heart attack. No warnings. No clues as to what was about to happen. Just went to bed one night and was dead in the morning. I didn't even know that anything had happened, was happening. Couldn't even comfort him and hold his hand when he took his last breath.'

'When was this?' I asked.

'Three months ago. I went through denial at first. Pretended to myself that nothing had happened. Did some stupid things. Totally irrational. Cooked for two, laid the table for two. Tea for two in the mornings.'

'Death affects people in different ways,' I said. 'I've seen it plenty of times from the other side. Denial is one of the ways of coping. The next stage is usually self-loathing – beating yourself up for all the things you wished you hadn't done and those you wished you had done while they were alive. Sometimes it's places you wish you had visited together. At other times it's something small, like wishing you had said "I love you" the night before they died.'

'How true,' she said. 'I've been there. Then reality hits. The admin, the paperwork, the forms to fill in. Each one a reminder of what you have lost. I've been going through those motions the last couple of months. And now, all the arrangements have been made. Technically, I'm back to being me again. Just me. That spinster has returned.'

'No, that's not true. You have simply entered a different state. You haven't regressed, you've moved on to a different life, not back to an old one. If you don't see it now, you will soon. Everything will become clear in a while. Too soon and you can't see the wood for the trees.'

'Cliché again,' she said, 'And it may be true, but you missed out a stage. Self-pity is next,' she said. 'I went through that, too. Still sink into it if I let my defences down. But I'm getting over it now. The healing will take its natural course.'

'But you still haven't answered my first question. Why here?'

'We always said we should come here for a holiday. Do some hiking, a little skiing, take a sailing boat out on the lake. It's a sort of pilgrimage for me. My last farewell to my old life. There's nothing to keep me in Poland anymore. In a couple of weeks, my affairs will be sorted out and I will return to England. God knows what will happen then, but it seems the right thing to do. Return to my roots. Draw a line over the past. But I shall miss Poland. The people are good here. They've been through a lot in the past and are forging a new identity. I would have liked to have been part of that.'

'Why not stay for a while and see whether you can adapt to a new life here? It would be a shame to throw it all away.'

'I'm not sure I could do it on my own. In England I could manage without support. Here, who knows?'

'Why don't you enjoy your holiday and see how you feel at the end of it?'

'Why does it matter to you what I do?'

'Decisions made in haste are often not the right ones. You have the perfect environment here to dwell on where you should be heading in life. Take advantage of it. Make sure you're taking the right course.'

'Do you always poke your nose into other people's business?'

'Always. Can't help myself. But if it's any consolation, things tend to work out fine in the end.'

'Why don't you get us a pot of that coffee you recommend and give me the chance of asking the questions. I want to know why you are here.'

'It's a long story,' I said.

'Then you had better get two pots of coffee.'

We talked for maybe forty-five minutes. At the end of which, she looked at me with narrowed eyes.

'Let me sum up,' she said. 'You kill people for a living.'

'No,' I said. 'I used to. Now I run a bar on a tropical island.'

'And that makes it all right?'

This was going to be an argument I couldn't win.

'What's in the past is done, but we never killed wantonly. Most of the time we only aimed to injure and put people out of the action.'

'How noble of you.'

'I like to think so. You've heard of Robin Hood and William Tell. We like to put ourselves in that class of freedom fighters.'

'I'm sure you do. But in Amsterdam, you say, you had two mafia gangs fight each other with several men killed on both sides. Didn't you find that excessive?'

'Can anything be excessive when you're talking about bad men? Men who kill without a second thought and who show no mercy? Those that live by the sword should die by the sword.'

'Another cliché. I think I have to reserve judgement on you, Mr Silver. A man must have values, and I need to see for myself if you possess them and in the right quantity. I only associate with the right kind of people.'

Must be a select group, I thought.

'We could probably arrange for you to have a ringside seat of the action, if you wish.'

'I hardly think that will be necessary. I shall do what I always do – consider the matter fully before I judge a person. Good day to you, Mr Silver.'

And with that, she left the table and walked as haughtily as she could in Ho's basic trouser suit. I would have to work hard to prove myself to her. Hell, what did it matter? I didn't need her assessment of me to point out the course I should take, in life or in Poland. I would do what I had to do. Some folks wouldn't like it, but others would benefit hugely. I finished my fifth cup of coffee and exited the restaurant.

While Stan was bringing the car around to the front of the hotel, I took a tour with Pieter in case I could help with firing positions. To the right of the entrance was the reception area, wooden counter with computer on a shining top, easy chairs, nothing out of place. To the left, the lounge where we had gathered last night. At the rear and to the left was the dining room, which looked out over the slopes of the hills. There were double doors which led to the terraced area where you could dine al fresco when the weather permitted it. Next to that was the kitchen, which also had a door to the rear and a fenced off area where deliveries were made, and the rubbish and recycling bins sat ready for collection. I didn't want to pre-empt Pieter's thoughts, but the rear looked like it could be defensible by two or three of us. The top floor of the hotel would make a fine look-out point, but not much good for a man with a gun – the angle was too oblique and anyone standing close to the hotel would be out of range and in a blind spot. It was the ground floor where we should marshal our forces.

Stan tooted the horn of his car and we went to join Bull and Red. We climbed in and Stan drove along the promenade and up a winding road into the hills. It took thirty minutes to get to the gun club. It was a long, low building with little style and lots of concrete, simply utilitarian, I guessed. From the front, I could see wide windows set at the bottom of the ground floor – that must indicate a basement, ideal for a soundproof rifle range for practice.

We were greeted by a man who was tall and thin, wearing round spectacles. He was dressed in faded jeans and a near-white sweatshirt. Stan went off into Polish, presumably explaining what we wanted. The man nodded and led us down a flight of stairs into the basement. There was a small office and a room with rifles in racks and handguns in two display cabinets. On the wall was a girly calendar from some supplier or another – impossible to guess of what as the girls very much had pride of place: we were two weeks into August, but July still smiled out in her low cut swimsuit and ultra-high heels. Whatever turns you on, I suppose. The majority of the basement was open plan and constituted the firing range. Targets were at the far end and were fixed to wires and pulleys so that you could wind the target back to the firing position for close examination. The man moved to the display cabinets to show us his wares.

'The only hand guns we have are Glocks.'

'The Glock 18?' Bull asked.

The 18 was a fully automatic and could be loaded with thirty-three rounds. It was a formidable weapon that was a favourite of police and security forces.

'No, the 17.'

Bull shook his head in disgust. The 17 magazine could only take seventeen rounds and was semi-automatic, making it slower for rapid fire than the thirty-three.

'That will have to do,' Stan said. 'We can't afford to be choosy.'

The man unlocked one of the cases and handed each of us

a gun. He went to a set of drawers stacked on the wall and took out two boxes of bullets.

'If you would like to follow me,' he said, moving to the fixed positions for firing. He gave out a handful of bullets and waited while we loaded up. He nodded his head as we did so, acknowledging the speed with which we loaded the guns. 'You guys look as if you've done this before.'

He offered us headphones to deaden the noise of the firing, but we declined. Hard men don't need headphones, so none of us was going to blink first and ask for a set.

I fired off six rounds and examined the result through a pair of binoculars that the man handed me. It was a good pattern, tight and centred just below the bull. I fired off another three rounds and wound the target back. The last three rounds were closer to the bull. I knew I could improve on this once I had got used to the gun. Red, Pieter and Stan followed my lead, each testing his weapon in turn. Bull just stood there watching us. Mr Cool, he took a strip of chewing gum from his jacket pocket and put it in his mouth. He chewed for a while, looking pensive. Finally, he stepped up to the mark and weighed the gun in his hand. He fired three times and shook his head. He wound back the target and examined the results. All a little too high.

'Gun's unbalanced,' he said, shaking his head.

He took the chewing gum from his mouth and tore off a small piece. He rolled it into a ball and fixed the ball on the underside of the tip of the barrel. He wound the target back to its position and fired three rounds again. Dead centre.

'Wow,' the man said. 'How did you know what weight to put on the end of the gun to get it in perfect balance?'

'You either have a feel for these things or you don't,' said Bull. 'It's not something that can be taught.'

'We'll take the guns,' Stan said. 'And one hundred rounds

of ammunition.'

'Of course,' said the man.

'Each,' said Stan.

'Wow,' the man said again. 'This must be some hunting trip you're having.'

'We'll also take five shotguns, but we want half the barrels sawn off.'

'I can do that while you wait,' the man said. 'Have some more practice while I do it.'

'I don't suppose you have any assault rifles?'

He shook his head. 'Not much call for them round here.'

Yet, I thought.

'What sniper rifles do you have?'

'I can do you a Zastava M76,' he said.

Made in Yugoslavia, it was a clone of the SDV Dragunov. The Dragunov wasn't as good as the Barrett M82A1, the monster sniper, so we were moving down two classes. The Zastava would have to do, but it didn't have the accuracy of the original or the power and effective range of the Barrett.

'How many have you got?' I asked.

'Just the one,' the man said.

'We'll take it, plus fifty rounds of ammunition. If you can start shortening the shotguns, we'll test the Zastava. We'll also take five shoulder holsters. Make us out a bill and I'll settle in cash.'

'I'll be back this afternoon,' Stan said, 'for another Glock and to give someone some lessons. Put that on our bill, too.'

We walked back to the range and loaded up the sniper rifles. When we were out of earshot, I turned to Bull.

'They fall for it every time, don't they?' I said.

'Never fails,' he replied, grinning.

'You purposefully aim high with the first shots and then do the trick with the chewing gum. Once that is in place, you aim properly. Bullseye.'

'Man's gotta get his fun somewhere.'

'Reckon so,' I said, smiling. 'Reckon so.'

We had a quick sandwich – rare roast beef on some sort of black bread with grains in it and the obligatory dill pickles, washed down by the light Polish beer – before Stan and Ho left to get in some familiarization and target practice at the gun club, and the rest of us grabbed hammers and nails and set about erecting the first of the mosquito screens. It looked easier than it was. The problem was the tension. We had to get it right – too loose and a Molotov cocktail would hit the windows and burst, too tight and there wouldn't be any bounce to take the bottles back from the window out of harm's way. We worked in pairs – one stretching the wire net until happy with the tension, the other hitting the nail at the signal to go – happily, we didn't do the when-I-nod-my-head-hit-it routine.

There were two problems, though, apart from the stretching. The first was that we could only work while the guests were out – didn't want the hammering to disturb them – so that limited us to finishing by around five o'clock. The second was that there were more windows than we had reckoned on. We would have to complete the job tomorrow – Saturday – when the weekend guests had checked out. It was going to be tight to finish before the expected arrival of the thugs on Sunday.

I was working with Red at the front while Bull and Pieter set about the back. Halfway through the afternoon, Mrs Freeman emerged, carrying a tray. She placed it very carefully on the ground like it was a precious object made of glass which would shatter if you breathed on it.

'I thought you boys might like some afternoon tea,' she

said. 'Made by me, no less, to my age-old recipe. The problem with this country is they don't get the water hot enough before adding it to the pot. Leads to a weak brew.'

'And we wouldn't want that,' I said.

'Certainly not,' she said. 'Tea should be strong enough so that you can't see through it. I brought you some scones, too. Just like Mother used to make.'

'Not like my mother,' said Red. 'My mother could burn water.'

Mrs Freeman bent down and poured tea from the pot into two china cups.

'Bought them this morning,' she said, seeing me look at the cups. She beamed at me. 'I'll lick this place into shape in no time.'

I wondered what Stan would think of that.

'How come,' I said, 'you are serving us afternoon tea? Shouldn't you be out walking or sailing or some such healthy activity?'

'Stan's girl didn't show up for her afternoon shift, so I volunteered to step into the breach,' she said brightly. 'Now, come along, boys. Tea will be getting cold. Just add milk and sugar to taste. Remember that the milk should go in after the tea, not before. It's up to us to maintain these traditions or they will die out. No excuse for being sloppy just because we're in a foreign land.'

This was the sort of attitude that built an empire. Trouble is, this was Stan's empire. How would he react to this invasion? Mosquito wire wouldn't be the only thing under tension.

'What's wrong with coffee?' Red asked when she had gone. He looked suspiciously at the dark brown mixture in the cup.

'Just that it's not tea. How can one have coffee at afternoon tea?'

'You're beginning to sound like her.'

'Not necessarily a bad thing.'

'Anyway, Comanches don't drink tea. Never have, never will.'

'You'll drink this cup, though. We don't want to offend her.'

'And I suppose I have to eat the scone, too,' he said. 'Whatever that is.'

'Wait till I tell Bull that I saw a Comanche eating a scone. You'll be in for some ribbing.'

'So what is she to you that we're making this effort?'

'She has just lost her husband – I feel sorry for her. And she's got values and tries to uphold them. There's a lot to be said for that.'

'Kinda like us,' Red said. 'Maybe I'll spend some time with her, too.' He took a bite of the scone and finished up with cream and strawberry jam smeared all around his mouth. 'Not bad. For white man's food,' he pronounced. 'No offence.'

'None taken.'

'We got company,' he said.

A blue and white striped police car came to a halt beside the burnt-out hotel. The door opened and a man in a smart, creaseless blue uniform with a gold braid on his epaulettes got out and stretched. He was obviously from the up end of the food chain and could be a useful ally. I put down the hammer and walked across to him.

He was tall and thin – like Caesar would have called a lean and hungry look, Cassius style. His face had a two-inch scar running from under his right eye. Badge of honour to go with the gold braid. This guy gave the impression that he had been everywhere and done everything.

'Afternoon,' I said.

'You're English,' he said.

'Did the lack of dill pickles betray me?'

'What?'

'Sorry. Never can refuse the opportunity to be a wise-cracker.' I stretched out my arm. 'Johnny Silver. Pleased to meet you.'

He shook my hand and regarded me for a moment, not sure what to make of me. 'Captain Vojek,' he said. 'What's your interest in this place?'

'My friend, Stanislav, owns the place next door – the one we're working on at the moment.'

'Did you see what happened?'

'Too late, I'm afraid. We arrived on the scene when it was burning badly. Did what we could, which was little.'

He seemed happy at this. 'Lucky no one was killed,' he said. 'I hope the owner has learned a lesson.'

'Excuse me?'

'Faulty electrics. Should have had the place rewired years ago. Too late now, of course. Insurance company won't be happy.'

'What do you mean faulty electrics? There was a bottle from a Molotov cocktail right outside this window. Rag in the top, too.'

'Some drunk dropped it, is my assumption. Rag probably his handkerchief. It happens. Still, the fire chief and I agree. Just came for one last look before I close the file.'

This was going to be a losing battle. The man had made up his mind, lubricated by a fat cash payment, I suspected.

'What are you doing to the windows?' he asked.

'Netting,' I said. 'Keeps the insects out. Nothing too good for Stan's guests.'

He shrugged. I was English so should be allowed my eccentricities.

'Don't expect I'll see you again, Mr Silver. Good luck with the insects.'

He turned and got back in his car. Rode off into the sunset.

'What was he here for?' Red asked.

'To apply whitewash.'

'Huh?'

'Whatever we encounter, we won't get any help from the police.'

'Situation normal, then,' he said.

'Reckon so.'

CHAPTER SIX

'YOU'LL HAVE TO do without me this morning, guys,' I said the next day.

We had just finished breakfast and were sitting back in our chairs contemplating the day ahead. As a special treat for Red and his American roots, Ho had made pancakes and, in the absence of maple syrup, had served them with honey. She was a treasure, thoughtful and resourceful, and Stan would be at a great loss if she ever decided to go back to Texas.

'So, just how come you're missing out on mesh duty?' Pieter asked.

'I have an appointment with a lady,' I replied.

'Anna's not going to like it,' Bull said.

'Anna would approve of this woman.'

'And what are you going to do with this woman that's so important that you abandon duty on the defences?' Red asked.

'I'm going to rally the troops. See if I can't get us some reinforcements.'

'Be a good trick if you can pull it off,' said Bull.

A figure moved up behind me.

'Come along, Mr Silver. Chop, chop,' Mrs Freeman said. 'You said nine o'clock and it's already three minutes past.'

'On this occasion I won't tell Anna,' said Bull. 'Don't want her knowing that you get desperate three days after you leave her.'

I rose from the table and turned around. Mrs Freeman was wearing a skirt and jacket in dark grey over a white blouse. She had a navy blue silk scarf around her neck and low-heeled black shoes with the shine that comes straight from the box and would be ideally suited to a sensible walk along the promenade. She was to act as my interpreter in case the hotel owners didn't speak English very well. Stan had told me that the young were better at speaking English as it was taught in all schools nowadays, but the older generation didn't have the advantage of that education.

My plan was to visit as many hotels, bars and restaurants as possible this morning and determine whether the owners felt strongly enough about the protection racket to join us in our fight. Maybe if we got enough of them to stand up and talk to the police, then we might be able to go over the head of the bent Captain Vojek and get some action. It wasn't something I was overly optimistic about, but was worth a try. If we could avoid bloodshed, everyone would be happy. If we couldn't, then we would be ready. Then whoever was behind the protection racket had better watch out.

'You'll stir a hole in that cup,' Mrs Freeman said.

I looked up at her, put the spoon down and shrugged my shoulders.

We were sitting in a pavement café, overlooking the lake and drinking coffee – mine short and black, hers, to my surprise, uncharacteristically white and frothy. We'd spent three hours trudging along the promenade, calling in at every hotel, shop, restaurant and café. Not one of the owners would stand with us against the protection racket mobsters.

'That didn't quite work as you had hoped, did it?' she said.

I gave her another shrug, not willing to admit to myself that she was right.

'Don't keep shrugging, Mr Silver,' she said. 'It can become quite irritating very quickly. You can hardly blame them, can you? Put yourself in their position. The fire has frightened off any resistance they might have made. It's safer for them to pay up than lose their whole livelihood.'

'I was hoping they might think in the long term. Ask the crucial question – can they keep paying the price and still stay in business?'

'Ah, the long-term,' she said with a shake of her head. 'I think it was Keynes who said, "In the long run we're all dead." Life is about short-term decisions and they seem to have made theirs.'

'So we're on our own,' I said. 'We've been in that position many times before. We'll pull through.'

'And how do you plan to do that?'

'One step at a time. Tomorrow the thugs will come round to collect their money from Stan. We'll have the element of surprise. Send them running home to Papa – whoever he turns out to be. They won't be used to losing. It will hit them hard.'

'And then?'

'Play it by ear.'

'I think it's my turn to shrug,' she said.

As we neared the hotel I could hear raised voices. I recognized Red's Texan twang and Stan's Polish monotone. Something had set off. I hoped it wasn't connected to Ho – Red trying to tempt her back to the Lone Star state, maybe – that could drive a rift between them and break a beautiful friendship.

Red was pointing at a small beat-up car parked at the kerb outside the hotel. It looked as if the only thing keeping it together was the rust molecules holding hands.

'What's got you both riled up?' I asked.

'Have you seen this?' said Red, sneering at the car. 'This heap! How am I ever going to follow someone in this? Be hard pressed to catch a snail.'

Stan threw him a bunch of keys. 'Look under the bonnet,' he said.

Red caught the keys and stared at them. 'Hasn't even got remote control,' he moaned. He unlocked and opened the driver's door and felt around under the steering wheel. Popped the bonnet catch. Opened it wide and propped it open. 'Jesus!' he said in wonder. 'How the hell did they get all of that in that small space?'

'I told you it was special,' said Stan.

'Is that a turbo charger?' Red asked.

'No, it's a super charger,' corrected Stan.

'What's the difference?' asked Pieter.

'A turbo charger only cuts in at a certain number of revs,' said Stan. 'A super charger is always active, no matter how low the revs. There's nothing on the road that can catch this thing.'

'Well,' said Red grudgingly, unwilling to back down from his initial assessment, 'I suppose it will do after all.'

'Where did you get it from, Stan?' I said.

'It's a project I've been helping with. Bunch of rejects from the local college. Something to do to keep them off the streets at night. Maybe even turn them into proper mechanics so that they can get a job rather than resorting to crime. Seems to be working, too.'

'You've done well,' I said.

'The sat nav's in the glove box,' Stan said.

'Why do I need a sat nav? I'm just following someone,' Red said.

'I thought you might want to come back. You know, like,

for old time's sake.'

'Comanche warrior can find his wigwam in the pitch dark. Can smell camp fire in the soft tickle of breeze, can follow broken twigs on trail, can put ear to ground to hear approach of enemy's horse.' He looked at Stan and smiled. 'But thanks anyway, Stan. Appreciate it.'

I gave a sigh of relief. All's well that ends well.

It was two o'clock in the morning and the start of my two-hour shift. Bull went inside as I came out and we high-fived to signal the passing of the watch from him to me.

We had dragged a high-backed chair from the dining room and a small coffee table from the lounge. On the table was a flask of strong coffee, mugs enough to last all of us the night, cream and sugar, and my Glock. On top of the Glock, for the purposes of discretion and in case Vojek popped round for a friendly chat on neighbourhood policing, was a Polish newspaper. I poured a coffee and went over the day.

The morning had been a disappointment, but Mrs Freeman was right – why should the local people risk everything when the power of the protection racket people had been so demonstrable through the burning down of the hotel? Maybe if we pulled off a victory or two, some would change their minds and move to our side. Whatever we might achieve, it would only be long lasting if everyone stood together.

The afternoon had fared better. The windows were all covered in mesh – Stage one complete. Stage two was trickier. How do we protect passers-by from getting hit in the cross-fire? The best we could think of at this stage was to use Stan's car and Red's beast as barriers parked on the promenade at each side of the hotel. After that, all we could hope for was that the sound of gunfire would scare anybody off. Maybe it wouldn't come to that, I told myself – and I didn't believe me.

There was hardly anyone on the promenade at that time. There were no discos, casinos or other types of late-night entertainment, although they might come in the future. For now it was a family resort, and pretty much everyone was tucked up in bed after exhausting themselves on the sports they had chosen. When someone did come past, they smiled and said what I took was 'nice evening'.

The sky was clear and the temperature had dropped. I had on a bomber jacket of black leather to keep out the cold and Ho's coffee for the inner man. I paced up and down every fifteen minutes or so in order to stretch my legs and retain my concentration. The danger when you are on watch is that your thoughts start to wander and you start to doze. It's the boredom that gets you and drags you down into the arms of Morpheus, as Mrs Freeman would say. I sat back down and poured more coffee.

There was the scrape of a chair from behind me. I turned around and Pieter dragged the chair next to mine.

'Mind if I join you?' he said. 'Couldn't sleep.'

'It's the calm before the storm. The night before the action. We all get a little jumpy around this time. All I think we do is imagine the scenarios that might develop and how we would cope with them. Mind keeps going round and round. Sleep's not easy.'

He nodded. 'Good to know it's not just me,' he said. 'Do you think it gets Bull the same way?'

'Hard to tell with Bull. Bull is unique. I've never met anyone as cool as Bull. But you see him back on St Jude with Mai Ling and little Michael, and he's a pussycat. For Bull, this is business – he can compartmentalize his life, there and here. If you had to choose anyone to stand beside you in a fight, it would be Bull. No offence, Pieter, but Bull's the best.'

'No offence taken,' he said. 'I'd go for any one of you to watch my back. But Bull has such a demoralizing effect on the opposition. He seems invulnerable, immortal even. You can see the fear in their eyes. It's like they're spellbound, staring into the eyes of the cobra as it prepares to attack. They're half-beaten before they start. Let Bull loose and all hell is unleashed.'

Pieter poured himself a mug of coffee and added sugar and cream. He took out a silver hip flask and poured some in the mug. Stirred it like I had done earlier with Mrs Freeman. His mind was on other things.

He looked at me and I nodded. He poured some into my mug and I smelt the vapour of Polish brandy. I took a swig. It hit the spot.

'We're a good group,' I said. 'Stan is our meticulous planner. With Stan, you know he's thought about every-thing in advance and planned for all eventualities. You feel that nothing can go wrong when Stan's around. Then there's Red with all his Comanche jibber-jabber. The craziest driver around, but he'll get you out of trouble faster than a rocket.'

'And me?' Pieter asked. 'Where do I fit in?'

'You're the ladies' man. You can't resist a pretty face. And you can fall in love with any woman you meet. You remind us that love still exists in this dirty world in which we live.'

'And you?'

'I'm just the glue that sticks us all together.'

'More than that,' Pieter said. 'You're our moral compass. You always do what is right rather than what is easiest. You'd never shoot a man in the back even if he had a gun pointed at you. Having to shoot those kids in Zimbabwe hit you hard. It went against the rules you play by.'

He took a long swig of his coffee and savoured the taste. He was quiet for a while. The two of us just sitting in a silence that neither of us felt was uneasy. I knew what he was thinking about.

'We'll have the element of surprise,' I said to reassure him. 'They won't be expecting trouble. And certainly not the quality of trouble that we bring. We're professionals. They won't have encountered the likes of us before.'

'And after tomorrow?' he asked.

'Ah,' I said. 'That's when it gets interesting.'

CHAPTER SEVEN

THEY CAME AT eleven o'clock. Four of them this time. Either taking no chances or combining to give a bigger beating than last time. The weekend guests had checked out and those staying longer were out enjoying the sunshine. The reception area was quiet and I could hear the sound of their heavy footsteps on the wooden floor. Stan was behind the desk and Pieter, Bull and I were spread around in easy chairs hiding behind Polish newspapers. Red would have the engine running on his car, ready to follow when we had finished with them. They disregarded us and approached Stan, a swagger in their walk.

Three of them were dressed in dark suits and white shirts as if going to Sunday mass – although that seemed highly doubtful – and one had a raincoat on. In this heat, it had to be a weapon he was concealing. We were ready for that. In contrast to them, we were dressed casually like tourists in chinos and T-shirts. The difference was that the T-shirts were worn loose outside so that our handguns, tucked into the back of our waistbands, were out of sight.

All four men looked like heavyweights, but some of the muscle had gone to fat, especially around their middle. They could still pack a punch, as Stan had found out, but they wouldn't last if the fight went on – they'd tire quickly, but I guess they never expected a fight to last long. Four against one sounded like good odds to them. The man with the rain-coat took out a baseball bat. We got up from our seats and walked slowly towards the group. We still didn't register on their radar. The man with the baseball bat tapped it into the palm of his hand as if to say 'bring it on'. He drew it back and prepared to take a swing at the computer on the reception counter.

'I wouldn't do that, if I were you,' I said.

He turned, looked at me hard and long and grunted something in Polish. Probably would have been much the same grunt in English, too. I didn't think his vocabulary extended much past grunts.

Then hell broke loose.

Stan leapt over the counter and attacked the man nearest to him, grabbing him by the throat. I faced the man with the baseball bat and Bull and Pieter squared up against the other two. What I knew, and the thug with the baseball bat didn't – thankfully – was that my left arm was weak and didn't pack much of a punch because of those bullets in Angola ripping apart the shoulder muscles. I needed to keep him on my right side and attack from there. He swung the bat and I leaned back. He was ponderous. The swing missed easily. He now tried the reverse swing and I jumped back this time. The swing missed me, but caught the arm of his friend who was standing to his right. I heard a bone crack – this guy was doing our work for us. While this registered with my opponent, I feinted with my left and, as he moved to block the blow, I caught him with a right hook and he staggered back under the weight of the punch. I moved forwards to close the gap and followed up with a straight right. I caught him on the nose, which is not good for the victim. If you are hit on the nose, your eyes water and your vision is blurred. I hit him again with a straight right and there was the grisly sound of his nose breaking. He didn't really know what was happening anymore. He made a lunge at me and I hit him in the stomach. He doubled up and looked like he was almost done for. I grabbed the baseball bat out of his hand and swung it up from floor level with a lot of force, straight into his groin. He let out another of his repertoire of grunts – this one higher-pitched – and fell to the floor clutching himself where it hurts the most. He was going to find it difficult walking, let alone terrorising the innocent.

I looked across at Pieter. His opponent was being hit by a combination of straight rights and left hooks. It was like Pieter was practising on a punch bag in a gym. Bam, bam, bam, bam. In the end it was only Pieter's punches that were keeping the man upright. Pieter stepped back and the thug slid to the floor.

Stan had stopped throttling his opponent and the guy was gasping for air. Stan hit him in the stomach, winding him even further. He followed with an upper cut and the thug was swept upright with the force of the punch. One more blow to the stomach and he slid to the floor, joining two of his workmates.

Bull had his opponent mesmerized by a series of slaps to both cheeks. They didn't cause much damage, but the effect was humiliating – this guy knew his time was nearly over.

'Don't play with your food,' I called across to Bull.

He looked across at me and smiled. Took a half step back and dropped his hands to his sides. The thug took a pace forwards and, half-heartedly, swung a punch at Bull. Bull, quick as a flash, grabbed the man's fist in mid-air. He squeezed. Hard. Very hard. The man sank to his knees with the excruciating pain and looked up at Bull imploringly. I heard the bones in his hand crack under Bull's pressure and then he let him go. It was over.

'Check their pockets,' I said.

They weren't armed, and that was reassuring in one sense, but if we came up against them in the future, they wouldn't make that mistake again. They were all loaded with money. Big wads of zlotys that they had taken from the other hotels, restaurants and shops. We passed it to Stan for safekeeping.

'Let's get them out of here,' I said. 'Red will be getting bored.'

We took a man each, dragged them across the floor and threw them casually out of the door as if throwing a bucket of slops into the gutter. They landed in a heap and lay there for a while gathering their wits. Clutching their wounds, they staggered to a black car and climbed in. Sped away in case we changed our minds and restarted the beatings.

'Remind me,' said Bull, 'why we didn't just beat the information out of them?'

'Because they could have told us any old baloney to get away,' I said. 'And I want the element of surprise again when we meet their boss. We need an edge when we meet them next.'

'Which will be soon,' Bull said.

'It will,' I said.

'Anyone for a beer?' asked Pieter. 'Beating thugs to a pulp is thirsty work.'

'Red might not like missing out,' Stan said.

'We could drink his share for him,' said Pieter.

'It's good to compromise,' I said.

'Ain't that the truth,' said Bull. 'Ain't done much compromising yet today.'

'We noticed,' I said.

'Boy, don't I feel a whole lot better after that,' said Stan.

'Amen to that, brother,' I said. 'Amen to that. Long may it last.'

It was an hour and three beers before Red came back. He had a wide grin that stretched from ear to ear and couldn't keep still, like he was high on something.

'Well,' he said. 'Don't I deserve a beer?'

'You tell us,' I said.

'You would have been proud of me,' he said. 'I kept three or fours cars back so they didn't spot me. Had to give the engine a burst a couple of times to pass a bus or truck to keep them in sight. Boy, can that wreck move!' He broke off to take a swig of beer. 'They went to a town about ten miles away.'

'That's Old Cezar,' said Stan. 'Been there maybe a couple of hundred years. Where we are now is all new buildings.'

'If we skip the geography lesson,' said Red, 'you might find this interesting. First stop was a hospital – four go in, only one comes out. That's the guy you hit in the balls with the baseball bat and he was walking like he'd been riding a horse for way too many hours.'

'He needs to put some ice on them,' Bull said. 'Ain't no other cure.'

'Thanks, Doc,' I said. 'Any words of advice for the guy whose hand you crushed?'

'Stay out of my way in future.'

'I think he's already got that message,' I said.

'Excuse me,' Red said, 'but I'm in the middle of a story here.'

'Pray continue,' I said.

'So the guy missing a horse goes on a mile or two and the car pulls up outside a modern building, maybe fifteen storeys high – must be some view from the top floor.'

'And then?' I asked.

'He goes in the building and I follow. He stays on the ground floor, walks past a reception desk and enters an office.

I try eavesdropping, but the door's too thick, so I go back out and sit in the car. Pretty soon three people come out – the thug, a man in a suit and what looks like a young boy – sixteen, seventeen, that sort of age. The thug drives off and the other two get into a flash black BMW 7 Series and speed off. They drive a couple of miles outside town and stop at a sprawling low house with gates and high brick walls – this is more like a castle or a fortress than a home, but that must be what it is. Nothing more for me to do, so here I am.'

'Well done, that man,' I said. 'Pass him another beer.'

Stan handed Red a bottle of the ice-cold Polish beer and Red took a long swig from the neck of the bottle. 'Funny, though,' he said. 'All the time I had this feeling that I was being followed.' He shook his head. 'Probably something to do with my Comanche instincts playing up.'

'What next?' Pieter said.

'We pay a little visit to the office and scare the man to hell,' I replied.

'And then we go home?' Red asked.

'It might be a bit more complicated than that,' I said.

'Reckon so,' said Bull. 'Might get to crush the guy's other fist.'

'That's what's great about you, Bull,' I said. 'You always look on the bright side.'

'So have you boys had a nice day?' asked Mrs Freeman.

'Nice?' said Bull with a wry smile. 'Yep, I think you could call it nice.'

We were sitting in the lounge, enjoying a pre-dinner vodka and planning for the next day's visit to Old Cezar. We all rose from our seats to acknowledge Mrs Freeman.

'I've been thinking,' she said to Stan. 'Yes, I *will* take the job.'

'What job?' he asked.

'The receptionist,' she said as if it all made sense. 'Well, she didn't come in again today – said she had the flu – well, we can't put up with such unreliability, so I had to let her go.'

'Oh,' said Stan. 'I see.'

The look on his face told us that it was obvious that he didn't.

'I think, however,' she said, 'that a better job title would be manageress, what with all the duties I would be performing.'

'Oh,' said Stan again. 'Manageress? Duties?'

I daren't look at Bull, who I reckoned was trying to suppress a laugh.

'Exactly,' she said. 'Now don't worry yourself about pay, I'll let you know that in the morning when I've had more time to think about it.'

'That's very thoughtful,' said Stan.

A slight snigger escaped from Bull's lips.

'And I insist that it is a one month trial,' she said. 'It's hard for me to see all the problems that may occur. But I guess we can climb over any hurdles and make it all work.'

Stan nodded. Bull got up and got a newspaper from one of the other tables and used it to hide his face in as the explosion of laughter within him was building to atomic proportions.

'One last thing,' she said. 'I think it would be better if you boys ate at seven thirty from now on so that we can concentrate on the peak demand for the restaurant, which I've noticed is always at its busiest at eight o'clock.' She gave Stan a smile. 'Well, that's all sorted then. Isn't this exciting? Now come along, boys, I've given you a table at the far end by the wall. We really should keep the window tables for the paying guests.'

She waved her hand in a grand gesture, motioning us into the restaurant. 'Chop, chop.'

We got up and walked meekly to the dining room and our allotted table. Bull joined us, shaking his head and pretending to have an itch on his cheek so that one hand covered his mouth.

'You might as well join us,' I said to Stan. 'Seeing as you are now redundant.'

We sat down and looked at each other, wondering which one of us was going to break first.

'Seems like congratulations are in order,' said Bull.

'What for?' said Stan in his most morose voice.

Bull gave a wide grin. 'You've just solved a problem that didn't exist.'

'And now I've got one that does,' Stan said, head in hands.

In the true spirit of camaraderie, four of us collapsed in laughter.

CHAPTER EIGHT

WE TRAVELLED TO Old Cezar in Stan's people carrier, which didn't please Red, who had become obsessed with what he called 'The Beast'. It didn't help either that Stan was driving. Red was a bad passenger. He couldn't keep his feet still, eyes darting about watching the road, shouting instructions to Stan and pressing an imaginary brake and accelerator to the floor. In short, he was as jumpy as hell and it made the rest of us twitchy, which wasn't a great prelude to what promised to be a crucial meeting with the bad guys.

Old Cezar was a bit of a misnomer: there *were* old parts with narrow winding streets situated slap bang in the middle of the town, but these had been unsympathetically surrounded by new blocks of offices and apartments, some rising to eighteen storeys high and dominating the skyline. It looked like the architect had been having a bad day when he designed it or maybe he needed a bigger fag packet on which to spread out his vision. It reminded me somewhat of Lisbon – the old town, the Alfama, in the middle and the new buildings radiating out from it. This wasn't a town anymore, it was a sprawling city.

The building we wanted qualified as what was a sky-scraper in Old Cezar – fifteen storeys high and built in a mixture of concrete and glass. It didn't look that old, but the concrete hadn't fared well – it was stained a dirty grey with pollution from the cars and had brown patches where the steel reinforcements had rusted and leeched out to the surface.

Red led the way inside and pointed at a set of double doors to the right of a reception area with a copy of a Polish celebrity magazine on the counter and, luckily for us, no receptionist – out for a comfort break or to get another low level of reading material. We approached the double doors and I silently turned the handle. The door was locked. I motioned to Bull, who stepped forwards and gave the door an almighty kick. The door locks sheared away and we made our dramatic entrance. I waved a pistol at the six people in the room and Stan shouted out an order in Polish to put their hands on the table and then not move a muscle. They froze like a tableau in a waxworks.

The room had been decorated by someone who had had their colour sensors surgically removed. The walls were painted battleship grey and were unadorned – no arty pictures, no photographs of family or distinguished colleagues and certainly no certificates boasting the owner's skill in some subject or another. At one end of what was a large room sat two black sofas and a black coffee table. The main table, around which our temporary prisoners were sat, was a rectangular black block of wood as impersonal as the walls. On the table itself was a laptop and printer and a thick tome, which I guessed was consulted from time to time when plotting the next moves in the world of crime. To add to the gloom in the room, the blinds looking out to the street were drawn tight and gave a claustrophobic feel to the environment. Why anyone wanted to work in this room baffled me, especially as I assumed Mr Big was rolling in money. I'd have spent it on a penthouse office with a stunning view across to the distant lake. You pays your money and makes your choice, I suppose.

The thugs who had taken a beating the day before were sitting with their backs to us at the table: opposite them, and facing us, were two figures dressed identically. The older one, taking centre stage at what I assumed was a council of war, was somewhere around forty. He was wearing a grey pinstripe suit with a white shirt and blue and red striped tie. He was clean shaven and had a dark complexion topped with greying dark hair cut short and brown eyes.

Next to him was a teenage clone – same clothes, same haircut, same eyes, same mindset, too, I suspected. Still, you shouldn't judge a book by its cover. My bet, however, was father and son. Dad looked up at me impassively, the lad looked scared – probably not been in this sort of position before.

'From now on we talk in English,' I said. 'Right, you four put your hands on your heads and slowly get up and move to the wall.'

The four thugs did as they were ordered and then the extent of their injuries was apparent. Two had plaster casts on the arm and hand respectively. One had tape running across his nose and the last one, who walked delicately, was covered in bruises all across his face.

I nodded to Bull and Pieter. They knew what to do. They frisked the thugs and came up with four handguns which they passed to Red. He took out the bullets from the guns, put them in his pocket and placed the guns on the table. He then took up a position against the doors, which had been closed to the best of our ability, to cover our rear. Bull searched the man and the lad and they were clean, then he and Pieter moved to opposite sides of the room so that we had them covered from every angle. Stan stood beside me.

'We need to talk,' I said. 'Or, rather, I talk and you listen.'

I picked up one of the chairs that had been so recently

vacated and pulled it towards me. I turned it round so the back was facing the two at the table and sat down straddling it with my arms resting along the back. I could feel Bull behind me suppressing a snigger at my stage-managed show of cool.

The man at the table said, 'You're a ...' He paused and pulled the tome towards him and started to flick through. It was now clear that it was a dictionary.

'I think the phrase you're looking for is "cocky sonovabitch".'

He nodded. 'I'm obliged to you. Now let's cut this short. What do you want?'

'I said that I'd talk and you'd listen. It will be your turn in a moment. Introduce yourself.'

'Emil Provda.'

'And the boy?'

'I no boy,' the clone piped up. 'I sixteen. Name Anton.'

'Well, Anton,' I said. 'There are some lessons to be learnt here. Do you want to hazard a guess?'

'Not ...' he consulted the dictionary, 'not *spare* enemies. Show no mercy.'

Dad nodded proudly and gave a thin smile.

'Wrong,' I said. 'Don't pick a fight with an enemy you can't handle. What happened yesterday was merely a preliminary to give you an idea of what we can do. It's not a sensible thing to pick a fight with someone who will beat you. And that is what will happen if you continue trying to extract money from the people of Cezar.'

'And what is it to you?' Emil asked. 'What interest do you have with all the people there? I'll tell you what I will do. I will let you off paying me money. Leave now and we will forget about it.'

'I'm afraid we can't do that. We fight not just for Stan and his hotel. We fight for all the little people who can't defend themselves.'

The boy looked puzzled as if it were a totally alien concept.

'Then we will fight,' said Emil.

'And you won't win. There's an ancient story about Leonidas, King of the Spartans, heavily outnumbered by the Persians at Thermopylae. When the Persians said that their arrows would blot out the sun, Leonidas said, "Then we will fight in the shade." We'll fight you in the shade, if needs be. In the end, we will take your organization apart, bit by bit and leave you with nothing. You have been warned.'

'Why don't you just shoot me?' Emil asked.

'Three reasons. Firstly, that's not our style. Secondly, we don't want Vojek on our back.' Emil looked surprised when I mentioned Vojek. 'And thirdly, well, it's better that I show you rather than trying to explain it.'

I pointed the pistol at Emil's head. Took aim. Squeezed the trigger. A stream of inky water hit him between the eyes. 'Explain to Vojek how five guys armed only with water pistols had you quaking in your boots. He looks like someone who could do with a good laugh.'

I looked at Stan. 'Take the laptop,' I said, 'and pay the man some money for it – we don't want to be accused of being thieves.'

Stan took out one of the rolls of zlotys that we had acquired from the thugs yesterday and counted out some on the table. Satisfied that it was a fair price, he picked up the laptop. I got up, nodded my head at the others and we backed through the door.

'We'll be seeing you,' I said. 'And, by the way, don't try burning down any more buildings.'

'What's to stop me?' said Emil with a grin.

'We know where you live and would feel morally bound to reciprocate.'

That wiped the smile off his face, but put one on the face of the boy who was still in fits of laughter from the water pistol incident.

We walked past the receptionist. She was engrossed in her celebrity magazine. If I'd been wearing a hat, I'd have tipped it at her. Would have made her day. Something to talk about instead of Victoria Beckham, perhaps.

We piled back into Stan's car and drove away. Half a mile up the road, Red turned around and looked out of the back window.

'What are you doing?' I asked.

'I'm getting that feeling again,' said Red. 'I can't see anybody, but my instincts tell me we're being followed.'

'Can you take evasive action?' I asked Stan.

'Hardly – we'll be back in ten minutes and there's not an alternative route.'

'OK,' I said. 'Keep watching, Red, and see if you can get something to substantiate that funny feeling.'

He turned around and took note of the cars behind us. There seemed to be nothing unusual – no sharp moves or jockeying for position. Maybe it was just his Comanche soul rising to the surface and spooking him.

'Can I ask a question?' said Bull.

'Fire away,' I said.

'What did we achieve by that meeting?' Bull asked.

'It was fun, wasn't it?' I said.

'Granted,' he said. 'But back to my question. What did we achieve?'

'We got a sight of what we're up against. Puts them into context. They're not faceless any more.'

'They don't seem scary now either,' said Pieter.

'Perhaps not. The problem will be who do they buy to beat us. They should know from today that they can't beat us on their own.'

'They'll go to Krakow or even Warsaw,' said Stan. 'Plenty of people short of money who would do anything and ask no questions.'

'So they'll buy in some specialists,' Bull said. 'And we'll fight in the shade. Right?'

I nodded.

'What happened to the three hundred Spartans?' Red asked.

'Dead to a man,' I replied.

'Shit,' said Red.

'Amen to that, brother,' said Bull.

There were two tables occupied when we went into the dining room, both of parents and young children yawning through a day's excitement. Stan had some music piped in – something classical that I didn't recognize, but was jolly in its tempo. The room had a good feel, not stuffy, an ideal place to relax – given the chance. We were sitting at our Mrs Freeman-allocated table in the restaurant at the Mrs Freeman-appointed time and waiting for Stan to join us. I hoped he wouldn't get a ticking off from her for being late – I'd sooner tackle one of Provda's thugs than her. Stan arrived, sat down, stretched his arms and rubbed his eyes.

'I think we should start calling Provda "Spreadsheet Man,"' he said. 'I must have waded through fifty or so on his laptop. I wouldn't be surprised if he didn't drink a cup of coffee without being part of a to do list on a spreadsheet.'

'I wish I could help,' I said, 'but Polish isn't my strong suit.'

'It's nobody's strong suit,' he said morosely. 'Why do you think we all have to try to learn English?'

Mrs Freeman walked up and stood over us.

'What would you like to drink with steak and salad tonight, gentlemen?'

'I thought I'd have a change tonight,' I said. 'There's only so much steak and salad a man can eat.'

'Me, too,' said Red.

'Oh,' said Mrs Freeman, sounding extremely put out. 'This is most irregular. I'll have to check with Chef.'

'With who?' asked Stan.

'With Chef. Miss Ho. I think it's only right that we refer to her by her title.'

'Would you like me to speak to Ho?' Stan pointedly said.

Mrs Freeman thought about it. Didn't like either of the alternatives. Relinquish her hold of the dining room or that in the kitchen.

'Just bring us some menus, please,' Stan said. 'And a couple of bottles of the Bulgarian cabernet sauvignon.'

Mrs Freeman gave a little huff and walked to the entrance to the dining room where the menus were kept.

'I will not be browbeaten in my own hotel,' said Stan.

'Time will tell,' I said. 'I wouldn't bet on it.'

'I'd recommend the roast pork with prunes,' said Stan.

There were nods around the table and Mrs Freeman brought the wine and deigned to take our order.

'Don't be too hard on her, Stan,' I said. 'She's lonely since her husband died. Hasn't really found a new role for herself. Give her time and she might find something to ease the pain and fill her long days.'

'The sooner someone finds a role for her the better,' said Stan. 'Don't let her see you have a soft side, Johnny, or she'll prey on it.'

'Physician, heal thyself,' said Bull and chuckled.

'The roast pork for all of us,' Stan said when Mrs Freeman arrived back at the table.

She looked at her watch. 'I think that will take a while to make,' she said.

'Then bring us some of the wild boar pâté and some bread,' Stan said.

'And some gherkins,' added Pieter.

'That goes without saying,' said Stan as he poured the wine.

Mrs Freeman departed and we relaxed. The wine was full-bodied and smooth – not the greatest in the world, but it went down well with the mood of the evening, once we'd resurrected it from Mrs Freeman's clutches.

'Did you really mean that this morning?' asked Red.

'Mean what?'

'About taking his organization apart?'

'Of course. We're going to take him apart at the seams until there's nothing left.'

'And why would we do that?' asked Bull.

'Because he's a bad man and bad men deserve all they get.'

'Wouldn't be because it's a challenge then?' said Bull.

'You know me,' I said. 'Would I do that?'

Bull looked around the table. There was a series of nods.

'I got my answer,' said Bull. 'Boy, do you know how to make life difficult, Johnny. But once you've got the bit between your teeth there's no stopping you. Well, master, what's the grand plan?'

'That depends on what Stan has found out from the spreadsheets.' I took some of the bread and spread some pâté on it, topped it with a slice of pickled cucumber. It was good. Meaty and strong. You didn't want to mess with this wild boar.

'Well,' Stan said. I sensed a long story coming. 'There appear to be four streams of business – protection, prostitution, smuggling of arms and, likewise, drugs. I sense he does the protection for fun and the rest is serious. His centre of operations is Old Cezar, as we know, but his field of operation extends to Krakow. Maybe he's based here because he likes the climate or something, and most of the revenue is from the city of Krakow.'

'How much are we talking about?' I asked. 'Did you get any sense of the size from the spreadsheets?'

'I've not had time to add together all the figures, but we're talking millions. Tens of millions, maybe.'

'Wow,' said Red. 'Manitou smiles on this paleface.'

I looked at him and raised an eyebrow.

'Jeez, Johnny. Only you would know that Manitou was Algonquin and not Comanche, but you getum myum drift?'

I nodded. 'We're going to wipe that smile from his face.'

'Are we biting off more than we can chew?' Pieter asked.

'Would it be worth it if we weren't?'

'I return to my question,' said Bull. 'What's the plan?'

'I'm working on it,' I said.

'Just how did I know you were going to say that?' said Bull. 'One thing we can say about you, Johnny. You're consistent.'

'What I don't get,' said Red, his brow furrowed, 'is if he's worth millions, then why is he bothering with a penny-ante protection racket?'

'Three possible reasons,' I said. 'Maybe just because he can – gives him a kick to throw his weight around. Like Stan said, it's a bit of fun. Second, he's a sadist and likes to see people squirm. That probably gives him fun, too. And third, it's part of a long-term plan. Think Cuba and the American mafia. The mafia invested heavily in hotels and casinos to diversify their worth. It's the same here. Cezar is going to be a boom town in the future – ideal for laundering dirty money and for a sound investment in the bargain. He'll buy up hotels and restaurants legitimizing his assets in the process.'

The pork arrived while we digested upon the personality of Emil Provda. It came with an apple jam, roast potatoes and bowls of vegetables – peas, carrots, broad beans and broccoli.

It looked good and tasted even better. The stickiness of the jam and prunes added a sweetness to the intensely meaty flavour of the pork. Stan said it was from rare breed pigs crossed at some point in the distant past with a wild boar, and that was why it tasted so different from the bulk standard pork we were all accustomed to eating. We fell silent for a while and it gave me time to think.

'I think I have some plans for the short-term – that is, tomorrow.'

'I suppose we have to settle for that,' said Bull. 'One day ahead is better than one day behind. We need to keep the element of surprise. There's not much else going for us.'

'You're starting to sound like Stan,' I said.

'Sometimes pessimism is a good starting point,' said Bull. 'Keeps you from making mistakes. But what have you got for us?'

'The first thing I need is a shoe mender.'

'Hell!' said Bull. 'This is going to get complicated, isn't it?'

'Stan, I want a shoemaker, or someone used to working with leather, to come here tomorrow and measure us up for leather gloves – as thin as possible so we can still have a delicate touch on the trigger.'

There were blank faces around the table. Red signalled Mrs Freeman for another bottle of red wine – he'd decided it was going to be a long night.

'The advantage,' I said, 'that Provda has over us is that the police are in his pocket, namely Vojek. We need to guard against Vojek being able to nail us for something. The gloves will keep fingerprints off the guns.'

Smiles spread across the faces. This was Johnny Silver the strategist working – Stan was our tactician, the detail man – I did the broad strokes, Stan painted the expressions on the faces.

'We also need to dum dum all our bullets. By doing that, cutting a cross at the point of the shell, the bullets will shatter when they hit something and make pinning down a bullet to a specific gun virtually impossible.'

I took a sip of wine – this was thirsty work. A brain often needs a stimulant to come up with the best ideas.

'Stan,' I said, 'can you translate the headings on the spreadsheets so that I can assess them, and how they might help us, in the morning. When you've finished that, go to Provda's house and make a detailed plan in case it becomes the final battle ground.'

Stan nodded and I could see him already making mental notes about how best to complete the task.

'Thirdly, we're stretched too far and will be more so when we take direct action against Provda. We need reinforcements.'

'Like unleashing Mrs Freeman,' said Pieter with a chuckle.

'I was thinking more of the Baker St Irregulars, the gang of youngsters who helped Sherlock Holmes.'

'Of course,' said Bull. 'Why didn't that occur to me?'

'Because you're the muscle,' I said. 'I'm the brains.'

'God help us,' he said.

'The youngsters who rebuilt the car, would they be up for earning some extra money?'

'If it's legal,' said Stan. 'I wouldn't want all the good work to be undone.'

'I want as many of them as you and I can persuade to patrol the promenade. We'll space them out so that we cover the maximum length. Whenever Provda's thugs turn up, they alert us. I was thinking klaxons. Make a chain of them, too – like beacons of fire lit one after the other. That way we can react quickly without being always on patrol ourselves. The klaxons might also stop Provda's thugs. Make them wonder what the hell is going on.'

'And what about the rest of us?' asked Red. 'What are we doing?'

'Bull and Pieter can pace out the promenade, work out where and how many bodies we need at any one time. You, Red, will be following Stan and me at a safe distance when we visit the garage. I don't like this funny feeling you're getting about being watched. I trust your instincts. Check it out. See if we are being followed and if so, by whom.'

'Can do,' he said. 'Comanche brave makeum good tracker.'

'And in The Beast you're unlikely to lose anyone,' I said. 'Time for coffee, gentlemen. We still need to guard against a night attack, although the odds on that have decreased somewhat since our meeting today.

'And a Polish brandy with mine,' said Pieter. 'I'm not on watch until four o'clock. The brandy will sharpen me up.'

'First time I heard that,' said Bull.

'You need to get out more,' said Pieter.

'Obviously,' said Bull. 'Any thoughts, Johnny, on our other problem? Mrs Freeman?'

'Not as yet, but I'll work something out. I'm getting a good feeling about this whole operation, but I won't tempt fate.'

'I'll have my brandy in the flask of coffee Ho will make for me,' said Red. 'I'm on first shift. Can't work out whether that's good or bad.'

'Simply regard it as necessary,' I said. 'Jump to it, lads. I've a feeling tomorrow will be a good day.'

'I'll drink to that,' said Pieter. 'But, on the other hand, I'd drink to anything. Success is better though.'

'Then I'll pray for that,' Stan said.

'Me, too,' the others said in unison.

I'd felt I'd covered all the angles. I'd raise a glass to that, too. Bring it on.

CHAPTER NINE

STAN AND I went to the garage of our 'irregulars'. It was on the outskirts of Old Cezar, so wasn't much good for passing trade, but someone could make a success of it, if given time to establish a reputation as being reliable, cheap and friendly. Stan told me that, at the moment, the garage was being subsidized by Old Cezar City Council, but it was hoped that it would shortly make a profit and finance itself and help to start up other projects. There were two qualified mechanics who provided the tuition and expertise and around fifteen youngsters, though not all at the same time, who provided the enthusiasm. Like Mrs Freeman, they had need of finding a role – to keep them out of mischief.

The four huge shutters were open to let air as well as cars and vans enter the premises. There was the din of power tools and the air was thick with exhaust and oil fumes – came with the job, I supposed. There was a car over an inspection pit and two people below it doing arcane things. In one corner was an old Volkswagen Beetle with its bonnet open and one man and three youths peering inside. This looked like the next project for transmuting into a beast. At the front of the second pair of doors was a white van with a name and contact details of a builder written in italic script. It was leaning to one side, although the tyre was fully inflated. This looked like one of those jobs where mechanics throughout Europe would

suck air in through their teeth and start tapping at a calculator. Three young lads and their instructor were sipping coffee
by it and debating what they could do to fix it. The instructor
looked up as we entered, saw Stan and gave a big smile.

The instructor was around fifty, plenty of experience
under his belt. He was medium height and showed the tell-
tale signs of a beer belly of a man who had taken a liking
to the Polish lager and not much of a liking to exercise. His
hair was dark and long, hanging over his forehead and ears
like a pair of facial curtains. His eyes shone with warmth as
he smiled at Stan. He said something in Polish to Stan, who
tilted his head in my direction.

'Forgive me,' the man said, switching to English. 'I didn't
know you weren't Polish. I was just saying to Stanislav that it
is always good to see an old friend and one who supports us in
our project. Will you have a coffee? How do you take it?'

'Black, please,' I said. 'As strong as you can make it.'

He raised an eyebrow and said, 'You asked for it.'

We followed him to a small room at the back of the garage
which was quieter and free from the fumes that pervaded
everywhere else. He took a coffee maker off an old stove and
poured three mugs.

'Fresh this morning,' he said.

I took the mug, added sugar and took an experimental sip,
expecting the coffee to be already stewed. I was wrong.

'Good coffee,' I said.

'The secret is good ingredients,' he said. 'Treat them
properly and you can't fail. Like the kids here. They're good
at heart – just need some direction from an understanding
mentor.'

'I suspect you're being too modest,' I said, 'but I take your
point. Without the right role model it's easy for kids to go
astray. Stan says you do good work here. I'd like to use some

of your kids' time and, in recompense, make a donation to your project. Maybe install some air conditioning, buy more or newer equipment, or just straight cash, if that helps you most.'

'Cash is always welcome,' he said. 'If we install air conditioning they might go soft and we wouldn't want that. What did you have in mind for them? Nothing illegal, I hope, because I'd like to help you. What you have to bear in mind is that these kids, and those like them everywhere, are the future. Our future. Our children's future. I wouldn't want anything to jeopardize that.'

'Me neither,' I said, thinking of Anna and the child to come – our future. I wanted there to be someone like this guy watching out for my child if anything happened to me. 'Trust me on that.'

He nodded. 'If you're a friend of Stanislav, that's good enough for me. What exactly did you have in mind?'

'Stan's been having some trouble. Him and all the other owners of hotels, shops, restaurants and bars along the promenade, maybe others, too, we don't know about yet. We need some help keeping a look out for some bad men who have been making threats and taking protection money. The area's too big to cover effectively on our own and we have other priorities, other plans.'

'Any risk to my boys?' he asked.

'Shouldn't be. We just need them to raise the alarm and then they can get the hell out of it. We'll handle any trouble from that point.'

He looked into my eyes and gave a shiver. 'I kind of think you will,' he said. 'You've got that same look as Stanislav. It says "Don't mess with me or you'll get hurt. Badly hurt." I reckon my boys will be safe with you.'

'We'll organize them into two shifts,' Stan said. 'Spread them out along the promenade to keep watch.'

'When do you want them?'

'We'll start this evening – some of your lads will have to work through the night. Might disrupt your business for a while, but we'll make it up to you.'

'You got a deal,' he said, extending his arm. 'Keep them safe is all I ask.'

We shook hands. We had our foot soldiers.

'You've got a visitor,' Mrs Freeman said to me when we arrived back. 'I told him I didn't know what time you would be back, but he insisted on waiting. I gave him a coffee – although a glass of warm milk might be better suited to his age – and asked him to sit over there.'

I turned my head in the direction she indicated and opened my eyes in surprise. It was the kid. Anton. Dressed today in a smart dark blue suit, white shirt and plain blue tie. He stood up as we walked towards him. He was taller than I'd expected from seeing him sitting down – one of those boys with long legs and an upper body that hadn't fully developed yet. He reminded me of a toy soldier decked out in all his finery. What the hell did he want?

'Can you get Bull and Pieter for me?' I asked her. 'Red should be along shortly. Maybe coffee for the six of us, too, if you can organize it.'

She nodded. 'I can set up a table in the dining room if you need somewhere less in the middle of things, somewhere where you can talk more confidentially.'

'That would be good,' I said. I turned to the lad. 'What brings you here, Anton?'

'Please forget me. My English is no good.'

Please forget me? Ah, he meant *forgive* me. This had all the makings of a very long and very confusing conversation. Mrs Freeman caught my eye and we decamped to the dining room. She'd laid out a table for six on the far wall and set it with two coffee pots, milk and sugar and a plate of chocolate biscuits. She smiled at me as we sat down, aware that she had done a good job. As she left us on our own, Bull and Pieter came in and did the same double-take that I had done just minutes earlier.

'What can we do for you, Anton?' I asked when we had sat down and Stan was pouring coffee.

'I want to know you. You are difficult.'

He wouldn't be the first person to say that. Then I thought again.

'Do you mean different?'

'Ah, yes. Different, that is the word.'

'In what way am I – are we – different?'

'You stand up to my father. No one do that before.'

'It just takes a bit of confidence and courage.'

'Courage? What is courage?'

'Try him with *balls*,' said Bull.

'Thanks for that contribution, Bull,' I said. 'I'm having enough trouble already.' I turned to Anton. 'Courage is being able to do something even though it might be frightening or dangerous.'

'Ah, yes. I understand. Where do you get this courage?'

'Pieter, would you like to tell him?'

'You find it inside yourself,' said Pieter. 'Sometimes it comes bit by bit from testing yourself, stretching yourself, sometimes it comes naturally in one move. Not everyone has courage and not everyone needs it. Courage is a part of the business we are in.'

'What is that business?' he asked, hopefully having understood at least part of what Pieter had said.

'We right wrongs,' Bull said. 'Protect the little people from injustice.'

'Why?' Anton asked. 'My father says that the little people are sheep and it's up to us to ...' he searched for the word.

'Shear them,' I said. 'I've heard that before and I didn't believe it then. It was said by a bad man who got what was coming to him.'

'And what was that?' Anton asked.

'Death,' I said, 'and that will happen to your father if he persists in what he is doing. Is that what you want?'

'No. How can I stop it?'

'By learning from us,' I said, 'and persuading him to stop what he is doing because too many people are getting hurt.'

'I don't know if he will listen.'

'Doesn't mean you shouldn't try,' said Bull.

'Tell me, kid,' I said, 'whose idea was it that you should come here?'

He faltered for a moment and said, 'My idea. It was my idea.'

I didn't believe him. 'Then we will let you watch us and talk to us about what we do and why we do it. If you see us in action, you will stand a chance of understanding what we do and why. Would that make you happy?'

'Happy? Yes, I want to be happy.'

'One thing we want from you in return. You won't fully understand what we do and our reasons when your English is so bad. You will take lessons and they start right now. Is that a deal?'

'A deal, yes. But where can I find someone to teach me?'

'Stan,' I said, 'can you think of anyone who fits that role?'

'I think I can,' he said.

'Then that's one problem solved,' I said. 'Call her in.'

He got up from the table and walked to the reception area. The boy watched him like a hawk as if he even wanted to learn how we walked.

ONE BULLET TOO MANY

Stan returned with Mrs Freeman at his side.

I got up and pulled another chair up to the table. 'We have a very important task for you. This boy needs to improve his English and at double speed. We want you to tutor him, starting right now. You will need to spend all your time with him apart from when he will join us for a meeting or a meal or when we have things to do that will benefit his education.'

'Reluctantly,' Stan said, 'I will have to ask you to drop everything and take on this very important new task. I don't know how I can replace you, but I must try to do my best.'

Out of the corner of my eye I could see Bull suppressing a grin.

'You can use my office,' Stan said. 'His name is Anton. Get him to tell you his story, his history – who he is and right up to how he came to be here today. I don't know how I can thank you enough.'

'Come,' Mrs Freeman said to Anton. 'We will start with tenses, then do some vocabulary. I'll have you talking like a native in no time.'

She stood up and gestured to Anton that he should follow her. They left the dining room just as Red arrived.

'What was he doing here?' he asked.

'He's going to do some ethnography,' I said.

'Is that good or bad?' Bull asked.

'He's going to shadow us and see what he can learn.'

'Why is he here?' Red asked.

'I suspect that it was his father's idea.'

'And why are we allowing him to do that?' Pieter said. 'I don't get what's in it for us.'

'Bull,' I said, 'tell him what you think is the reason he is here.'

'Know your enemy,' Bull said. 'At the moment, Emil can't

work us out. We beat up his men, but don't kill them. We walk into his office and threaten them with just water pistols. He tries to bribe us and we refuse to be bought. These are all situations he hasn't encountered before. Until he can work us out, he feels he can't produce a plan of attack.'

'But doesn't he fear that we would just kidnap his son?' Red asked.

'If we wanted to do that, we could have taken him from the office,' I said.

Red nodded. 'So what do we get in return?' Red asked.

'Think about it,' Bull said.

'Ah,' Pieter said with a broad smile. 'I get it. Brilliant! Know your enemy!'

'Bingo!' I said.

CHAPTER TEN

THERE WAS SILENCE for a while. Maybe a minute at most, but it seemed like a whole lot longer. Bull had the start of a smile on his lips and I guessed what game was being played. Finally, when no more tension could be squeezed out of the moment, Red said, 'Well. If we're finished with all this self-congratulatory diddly-squat, doesn't anyone want to know what I've found?'

Pieter yawned and said, 'Maybe later. Thought I might take a nap before dinner. I need my beauty sleep.'

'Sounds like a good idea,' said Bull. 'Conserve energy that might be needed later.'

It was time I joined in.

'I need to work on these spreadsheets with Stan,' I said.

'So,' said Red, 'a man drives around all morning, confirming that we got a tail and no one is interested?'

'Got to get your priorities right,' said Bull.

'Show some mercy, guys,' I said with a sigh. 'OK, Red, tell us what you found out.'

'The guy is waiting a little way back from Stan's car and follows as soon as Stan pulls away. He sticks with you and watches what you do at the garage. Picks you up again when you go to Emil's house and follows you back here. He must have guessed you'd finished for a while, because he moves off and heads to a hotel just up the promenade. Can't pronounce the name so I wrote it down.'

He handed Stan a piece of paper.

'I know it,' said Stan. 'Not much different to this one, but longer established. Comes out well when you search on Google. Sensible choice.'

'So then,' Red said, 'I park up and follow him inside, ten or so paces behind so I don't register.'

'And then you pull the Mr Smith trick,' I said.

'Yeah,' said Red. 'Except I didn't use Mr Smith.'

'So how creative were you?'

'I used Jones.'

'Wow, that creative,' I said.

'Anyway,' Red said, confirming that Americans don't do irony. 'I go up to reception and say, "Was that Mr Jones?" And she says, "No, it's Mr Leclerk." "Of course," I say. "I'll leave him a note." So I borrow a piece of paper, scribble something on it, fold it up and hand it to the receptionist. She turns round and puts it in cubby hole twelve. Now I know his name and his room. Next, remove the evidence. "Sorry," I say. "I think I'll ring him instead. No need for the note." She hands it back to me so he doesn't have a clue that anything had gone on. Pretty smart, huh?'

'I'll put him on my list of things to do,' said Stan.

'Soon gonna need another piece of paper,' said Bull. 'We're stretched, man. Fighting on too many fronts. Next thing you're gonna say is we split up, divide our troops. Never a good idea.'

'This afternoon,' I said, 'Stan and I will work on the spreadsheets, put together a plan of action.'

Stan nodded his head.

'You guys,' I said, 'will walk around the promenade. Make our presence felt. Give the bars and restaurants a bit more confidence. Try to look menacing.'

'Typecast again,' said Bull, shaking his head. 'One day you're gonna let me play the geek.'

'Not in my lifetime,' I said.

'May not be very long,' he said.

Stan and I sat at a table in the empty dining room, staring at the screen on the laptop. There were six spreadsheets of interest. The first four fed through to the fifth, consolidating the individual figures. The sixth was the least interesting from our point of view – it was the official accounts of the legitimate business. Income came from rentals on a property portfolio consisting mainly of office premises, shops and some residential apartments. Expenditure was mostly refurbishments and repairs. Profit was good, but unspectacular – probably artificially low to save on tax. I suspected there were a lot of cash payments unaccounted for.

The first spreadsheet was labelled "Prostitution" and the first column – almost entirely female names and giving the game away if the label hadn't been there – must have been the hookers. The second column was weekly income by prostitute, allowing Emil to check up on who was not pulling their weight. The third column was the pimps, a ratio of about twenty hookers to one pimp. They were concentrated in three geographical areas, all – according to Stan – seedier districts of Old Cezar. The fourth column was income by pimp with a grand total income at the bottom. It was staggering. I looked across at Stan and he raised an eyebrow – a massive reaction for him. He tapped away at a calculator, converted it to sterling and wrote a figure on a pad. Emil was making around ten thousand pounds a week after the payments to the pimps. Time to move on to the next spreadsheet. Protection. Small beer by comparison, but it was a new stream of business for him and the profits would come in the future when he had a virtual monopoly of hotels, bars and restaurants which were laundering his dirty money.

Moving on a spreadsheet brought me to gunrunning. Still in its infancy, it seemed. Purchases were high, but sales were disappointing. Well, I imagined that was how Emil would put it if he were CEO of a major company reporting to its share-holders. It wouldn't take much, I suspected, to persuade him to close down that niche market and concentrate his energies on his core businesses.

The fourth spreadsheet was drugs and there was an extra column giving receipts in various currencies, the biggest being euros and sterling. The drug income made prostitu-tion look like it was petty cash. The numbers we were talking about were huge. His empire must have been worth at least ten million and growing with every trick, punch, hit and bullet. Stan looked at me and raised his eyebrow a millimetre higher.

'Bigger than we thought,' he said. 'I have a nasty feeling we may have bitten off more than we can chew. Too big a pickled cucumber to fit even the largest mouth.'

'Not if you take it bite by bite,' I said. 'Let's get ready to start tonight. Can you get us a map?'

He minimized the spreadsheets and logged on to the inter-net. Brought up Google Maps and zoomed into Old Cezar. He pointed at the screen to show the three areas where the pimps were operating. One was on the verge of an industrial estate and had lots of open ground. That had to be the first, in order to negate the lack of cover by the element of sur-prise. Another was in a residential area and was surrounded by high rise flats: again, too little cover – that would be the second. The third was in the old part of the city, nestling in the maze of narrow alleys. That was perfect as the third. I told Stan the plan and left him to sort out the tactics.

'One thing is puzzling me,' he said. 'Lots of details over the income, but where is the money going? We haven't found anything that looks like a list of bank accounts. Where is he hiding it all?'

'Maybe Anton will help us out there. Let's get him over-confident and see what he will reveal. With any luck he will want to brag about it. Show us just how clever his father is.'

'Are you planning to let him come tonight?'

'Time we impressed him again. Let him see Bull in action.'

'OK. I'd suggest Pieter replaces Bull tomorrow. I'm getting the feeling that he's jumpy for a fight. Best not let him stew.'

Mrs Freeman walked through the door to the dining room and up to our table. She looked like she had just gone through ten rounds with Muhammad Ali. She lowered herself into a chair and sighed.

'Not going well?' I asked.

'His vocabulary is quite large, but not much of it is print-able. I had to wash his mouth out with soapy water.'

'You what?' I said, stunned.

'I washed his mouth out with soapy water. Old family remedy. That will teach him. He won't be doing any swearing again in my company.'

I shook my head in disbelief and then smiled. Maybe we need more Mrs Freemans to teach the young some moral values.

'Where is he now?'

'I left him in the lounge making phone calls – he seems welded to his mobile phone. Thought it was time for a break. For both of us.'

'What did you find out about him?' I asked.

'Strange boy,' she said. 'Thinks his father is God – all pow-erful, all seeing, all knowing. If you want to get through to him, you will have to disabuse him of that perception.'

115

'I'll work on it,' I said. 'Everybody has a weak spot. All we have to do is find it.'

'There are extenuating circumstances for the boy,' she said. 'His mother died giving birth to him. I've come across it once before. It sets up lots of problems for the surviving child. It can easily screw them up. Either the father blames the boy for his wife's death and punishes him constantly, or the father gives all that he has in raising the boy. I suspect you have the latter case. Anton has become completely immersed in his father. No other role model to copy. That's probably why Anton was taken out of school. Too risky. You could lose the control over the boy. Control of his emotions and his beliefs.'

'Poor kid,' Stan said. 'What a burden to carry.'

'We need to make him autonomous,' I said. 'Give him his independence. Sever the link with his father.'

'And replace it with us?' Stan said.

'No. That's not what autonomy means. He has to become his own person.'

'Admirable motive,' Mrs Freeman said. 'And all in a week or so. Would be a great achievement if you manage to pull it off.'

'We can but try,' I said. I looked at my watch. Twelve fifteen. 'Let's take a break. Have a beer and then some lunch. After that, Anton goes shopping. Make our first foray into changing his character. We'll have him back for you by three. Then you can work your magic again, Mrs Freeman. Show no mercy.'

'You asked for it,' she replied.

'Don't I always?' I said.

I left Anton with Bull, Pieter and Stan to have lunch while Red and I got our guns and then went for a walk. Our destination was the hotel where Leclerk was staying. Except we didn't get that far.

Red spotted his car immediately. It was parked up on the promenade where he would have a great view of the door to Stan's hotel. I motioned Red to take the driver's side and I went round to the other side. I opened the door and pressed the gun to Leclerk's head.

'Put your hands on your head,' I said, getting into the passenger seat. Red took the back seat behind me. He pointed his gun at the back of Leclerk's head. We had him covered from all angles. 'Don't move a muscle, pilgrim. My friend has very itchy trigger fingers and I'm not much different.'

'My wallet,' Leclerk said in perfect English.

'We don't want your wallet,' I said. 'We want to know why you have been following us.'

'Inside left pocket in my jacket,' he said. 'Take it out and look inside. That will explain everything.'

I switched the gun to my left hand and delved into his pocket with my right. I found the wallet and took it out. Then flipped it open.

'Shit,' I said, risking my mouth being washed out with soapy water if Mrs Freeman ever got to know. 'You can relax, Red.'

I showed him the wallet with its badge inside.

'Europol?' Red said. 'What the hell is Europol?'

'You've heard of Interpol?' Leclerk said.

'Course I have,' said Red. 'What do you think I am? Some kind of savage?'

'Europol is the European equivalent of Interpol. We're based in The Hague, but we've got agents covering the whole of Europe.'

'You better explain yourself,' I said.

'I'd like some answers from you first,' Leclerk said.

I looked at him and shook my head. 'You have two bad-tempered guys with guns sitting in your car. That doesn't give you much bargaining power.'

'The badge is my bargaining power,' he said.

'For the moment I'm trying to forget the badge. Tell me your story. And it better be a good one or my gun goes to your head again. Why have you been following us?'

'Can I take my hands off my head?'

'Feel free,' I said.

'Why don't we go inside and talk in comfort?'

'Because I suspect there's someone I don't want to overhear your story. Drive to your hotel and we'll go in there.'

He drove slowly along the promenade and parked outside his hotel. We entered and a receptionist gave a cheery, "Good afternoon." The hotel was similar to Stan's except the owners had gone for pine instead of oak. It made the lounge look lighter and more contemporary, but lacked that warmth of old-fashioned charm. You pays your money....

Now that Leclerk was out of the car, I could get a good look at him. He was short and rotund, maybe in his fifties and wore large round glasses of a high prescription so that when he looked at you he resembled an owl peering out at the world wisely. He could have been your favourite uncle before he gives you a caramel boiled sweet. This wasn't a man of action. He was a thinker used to operating behind a desk. His suit was dark blue and his collar seemed too tight for his neck so that his face had a flush. He was the kind of guy that gave you the impression you could confide in him, which I suspected I was going to have to do.

The lounge was empty so Red and I moved across to a table by a front window where we could see anyone enter from the front or back of the hotel. Leclerk was busy negotiating something with the receptionist which involved some arm waving and Gallic shrugs. Red and I took the two chairs facing out into the room, leaving the best seat – the one facing the window with the fantastic views of the lake for Leclerk. The receptionist stepped out from behind her desk on black high heels to reveal a dark grey skirt to contrast with her white blouse. Leclerk waddled over to us.

'Just ordering some wine,' he said, taking the seat with his back to the window. So much for being polite and leaving the best seat for him to use.

'What's with the wine?' I asked. 'Your birthday or something?'

'Any occasion is worthy of fine wine. Wine is a celebration of life,' he answered. 'If you were going to kill me, you would have done so in the car or had me drive to somewhere deserted. So I celebrate.'

'Why would we want to kill you?' I said.

'Ah, that was the question.'

'White man talk in riddles,' Red said. 'Too much for a Comanche brave to understand.'

'I think you should start at the beginning,' I said. 'What is Europol doing in Poland and what is your interest in us?'

He saw the receptionist bring the wine and glasses, shooed her away before she could pour it and then did it himself – this was a man low on trust. He took an experimental sip and smiled.

'Right,' he said. 'As you now know, I work for Europol. I am one of the officers in its Eastern Europe team. For the last few months, I have been getting reports from several European countries of new shipments of illegal drugs coming across their borders. They have made some arrests, but these have all been what we call Smurfs – little people far removed from the bosses. From the information gained by the arrested people, we know that the drugs originate from Poland and specifically the area around Lake Cezar. After much digging, I have uncovered the name of one Emil Provda, with whom I know you are acquainted.'

'I wouldn't put it quite like that,' I said. I took a sip of wine. Rich in berry fruits and it sang on the tongue. The guy had good taste.

'I tried to get the help of the local police, but they said Provda was a well-respected businessman.'

'The police officer who said that wasn't called Vojek, was he?' I said.

'Ah, you know him, too.'

'Again, I wouldn't put it like that. We've crossed swords.'

'And so, I decided to come here myself and see what I could find out.'

'So where do we come into it?' I asked.

'I spotted you straightaway. You don't exactly keep a low profile.'

'What do you mean by that?' I said.

'The fire,' he said. 'The way you rescued that old lady. The way you were organized. Knew exactly what you were doing. I can spot professionals a kilometre away.'

'And what did you deduce?' I said.

'I decided to look into what you were doing here. Seemed too much of a coincidence that there were five professionals a stone's throw from Provda. And what happens when I follow you? You go straight to Provda's office. You are connected to him.'

'Sometimes two and two don't make four,' I said. 'The connection wasn't the one you assumed.'

'So, enlighten me,' he said.

So I told him. Everything. Why we were here and what we intended to do. He sat back, took another sip of wine and nodded his head.

'So you intend to close Provda down. Take him apart.'

'Sure do,' Red said. 'And we'll enjoy every moment of it. Starting tonight.'

Leclerk raised an eyebrow. 'What do you have planned for tonight?'

'Hell!' Red said. 'Did I just putum big foot in ummouth?'

'It depends,' I said. 'Are you for us or against us, Leclerk? Will you help or hinder?'

'Officially, I must advise you not to take the law into your own hands.'

'And unofficially?'

'Cut him up in little pieces and throw him to the sharks.'

'I'd hate to get on the wrong side of you,' Red said.

'And you'd better believe it,' said Leclerk.

'What support do we get from Europol?' I asked.

'Me,' he said.

Red looked me. He had come to the same conclusion. I nodded my head.

'Are you flying solo on this one?' Red said.

Leclerk took a nonchalant sip of his wine.

'What do you mean by that?' Leclerk said, taking another nonchalant sip of wine.

'Are you here officially or is this a one-man crusade?' I said.

The nonchalant sip became a splutter.

'I take that as the latter then,' I said.

'Hell,' said Red. 'The last thing we need is a passenger sitting on our tail and getting in the way.'

'What did you say about bargaining power, Leclerk?' I said.

I thought about having a nonchalant sip of wine, but reckoned that was overdoing it.

'I don't like someone slipping through my fingers,' Leclerk

said. 'I can use my contacts to get information that might prove useful to you. Are you sure you can do this on your own – the five of you, that is – without any outside aid?'

'I think we see it less like aid and more as interference,' I said. 'Let's get a few things straight. We'll tell you what we're going to do and you keep out of our hair. If we need help, we'll ask for it.'

'And stop following us around all the time,' Red said. 'It makes the hairs on the back of my neck prickle.'

'So what am I supposed to do?' asked Leclerk.

'Take a boat out on the lake,' I said. 'Cruise about. Go around the island. See if you can spot any rare birds. Lie on the beach. Catch a few rays. Trek though the hills. Basically, anything that doesn't involve you getting under our feet.'

'Is there anything you'll let me do?' he said.

'Yes,' I replied. 'Buy another bottle of that red wine.'

CHAPTER ELEVEN

WE SET OFF just before eleven on a night with a crescent moon and a slight breeze blowing from the mountains. On any other occasion, it would have been idyllic, but romantic and picturesque were the last things on our minds. I sat in the front of the car with Stan; Bull and Anton made an odd couple in the back. Anton seemed so small alongside Bull, even when Bull was sitting down. Standing up, there was more than a foot between them. If Anton suffered an injury tonight, it would be a stiff neck from constantly looking up.

We were all dressed casually, although that was always the order of the day with us – you need to feel comfortable in our game. We had put on bomber jackets to hide our guns. By contrast with us, Anton's clothes were so new and pristine that he wouldn't have looked out of place on a catwalk.

The journey was short and none of us was up for much conversation. There was a battle ahead and we were all within ourselves thinking about it, trying to second-guess likely responses and how we should counteract them. Anton, who had nothing to worry about because if things went bad he could claim family immunity, had developed a nervous cough which I knew would become very irritating if he kept it up for the whole journey.

'Relax, kid,' I said. 'We're here to protect you. Stick close to us and you won't come to any harm. Anyway, we have the element of surprise, unless you've been blabbing to Papa, that is.'

'What chance did I have of that?' he said gloomily. 'And don't keep calling me kid.'

'I'll stop calling you kid when you behave like a man. If you ever do.'

'Can anyone join in the bickering?' Bull said. 'Or is it by invitation only?'

'We're coming up to it now,' Stan said.

'Thank God for that,' said Bull.

We pulled off the main road. It was a soulless place. The buildings all looked like aircraft hangars crafted from concrete with corrugated iron roofs. I'm sure someone must do worthwhile work here, but it was still a blot on the landscape. For the prostitutes, it provided an open space where they could stand in relative safety under streetlights peddling their wares, and there were points of shelter between the buildings where those who didn't want to soil their car could stand while being serviced. You'd have to be pretty desperate, but that's the market, I suppose.

My thoughts flashed to Anna, who had escaped from this oldest profession, albeit that hers had been the most upmarket you could get. I'd phoned her every day to check on how she was doing. I'd also talked to Gus, just in case she'd been hiding anything from me so that I wouldn't have my mind clouded by other things when there was danger before me. All was going well, although she had seemed somewhat distant when I had last phoned. Maybe she was missing me as much as I was missing her and was trying to keep her emotions in check. All in all, it had been an unsatisfactory phone call.

We parked up away a little to assess the situation and so as not to alarm the girls unduly. There were four that we could see from this vantage point, although we knew from the spreadsheets that there must be twenty or so in this area, unless they worked in shifts. The odd car passed us from time to time, picking up a girl and driving on. What a way to make money. I wondered how their pimp, wherever he was, could protect them from a crazed customer or serial killer while they were a virtual prisoner in a car.

Stan got out and the rest of us stayed hidden in the car. It was important not to scare the pimp. He walked across to where a blonde girl in a black mini skirt, sleeveless top and a mega pair of heels was leaning against the wall of one of the industrial units. I couldn't see from this distance, but had a bet with myself that she was chewing gum with a vacant expression. Stan's job was to get her to summon the pimp. We sat and waited. Anton started drumming his fingers against the leather of the seats. It was as annoying as the coughing. I bit my lip – can't be on his back all of the time, otherwise he wouldn't listen when I said something important – and looked at my watch.

We could see Stan and the girl talking, and then she pulled out a phone. It took five minutes for the car to come screeching to a halt. We got out of the car just as he stopped alongside Stan and the girl. Before he knew it, he was surrounded. He shook his head. This wasn't in his script.

He was maybe thirty, around six feet tall and obviously spent a lot of his spare time in the gym. There was muscle there, but did he know how to use it? The sleeves of his grey lightweight jacket were stretched over huge biceps. Probably took steroids, too, in addition to lifting weights, maybe practised, too, on the heavy bag. Fancied himself as someone who could handle whatever trouble life had in store for him. If he was fazed by us, he hid it well. I admired him for that. I wondered how long his act would last when Bull got going.

'You speak English?' I asked.

'What has it got to do with you?' he said, answering my question.

He looked at Anton and seemed bewildered. What was a kid like this doing out at this time of night? I knew what would be going through his mind. The kid was the weak point. If he could grab him, he had us neutralized.

'You're going to have to find a new job,' I said.

'You taking over, are you?' he said. 'We could reach a deal. You don't give me any trouble and I won't give you any.'

Loyalty wasn't his strong suit.

'We're shutting down your shop,' Bull said. 'We can do it easy or we can do it hard. You choose.'

He knew he was beat as soon as he looked into Bull's eyes. It was the look we all had. We have killed and will kill again. In cold blood.

He did the predictable. Made a grab for Anton and had his arm around Anton's throat before he spun back to look at us. Smiled.

'You better go,' he said, 'or your kid gets it.'

'I'm not a kid,' Anton protested.

The boy had some spunk after all.

'Teach him a lesson, Bull,' I said.

Bull took out his gun and held it casually. The pimp looked shaken. Would the black man shoot while he had the kid? That was what was going through his mind and he couldn't compute it.

'We explained it to you,' Bull said. 'We told you nicely that there's no role for you in the future.' He paused for effect. It worked. The pimp backed away a few feet. That wasn't going to save him. He could back away fifty yards and the result would be the same.

'What would you do in this situation?' I asked Anton. 'Time for another tutorial.'

He shook his head.

'What are our assets?' I said.

'There's three of you. You outnumber him. But he's got me. You can't shoot because you might hit me. It's a ...'

'A stalemate. A Mexican stand-off. I don't think so,' I said. 'You missed out one of our assets. We've got Bull. So now what are you going to do?'

'Are you going to kill him? Is that what you want me to say?'

'That's the last resort. We can take life but we can't give it. What would you do?'

'Sacrifice me. Shoot him. It's the only course of action.'

'Show him the answer, Bull,' I said.

'We asked you nicely and you didn't listen,' Bull said. 'Time it was that you had the tutorial lesson. One you will never forget.'

The pimp tightened his hold around Anton's throat. He didn't get it either.

It was like watching a ballet by the best dancer ever. There was something artistic about it. It was hypnotizing. With minimum effort and the speed of a trained athlete, Bull swung his gun up and fired twice. Each bullet hit the pimp's ears. He screamed. So did Anton as blood splattered down on his new jacket. The pimp let go of Anton and reached out to touch his ears. They weren't there.

CHAPTER TWELVE

ANTON WAS SHAKING when we dropped him off at the house at the end of the evening and was still shaking when he arrived at breakfast. He tried to look at all of us, but his gaze kept returning to Bull. It was shock and awe. Bull poured him a coffee and slid along the table. Anton looked at it as if it were a poisoned chalice.

He was wearing one of the new outfits that he had bought the day before – designer blue jeans with a light blue polo shirt, a short denim jacket and trainers. He might have looked cool except he had the top button of the shirt in the second buttonhole so that the collar was askew. It was a gestalt thing. He hadn't got the essence of the smart-but-casual clothes, didn't feel it. Maybe he was born in a suit and nothing else felt right to him. Ingrained. Changing him, maturing him, teaching him right from wrong was going to be harder than I thought.

'So what did you learn last night?' I asked him.

'I no know. I confused.'

'Tell him, Bull,' I said.

'The lesson, kid, was that sometimes a whisper can be more effective than a shout. What do you think the talk on the streets is going to be this morning?'

Anton still looked bemused. I had to put him out of his misery.

'You don't have to kill somebody to make your point,' I said.

Anton nodded. 'I see,' he said. 'So when do you kill?'

'When it's the only available option,' I said. 'Him or me. Them or us. Kill or be killed.'

'How many men have you killed?' he asked.

'Too many,' I said.

The others nodded their agreement.

'My father would kill,' Anton said. 'He will kill you all if you do not stop.'

'Many have tried,' Pieter said. 'So far, none have succeeded.'

The superstitious ones among us touched the wood of the table.

'He will send for men from Krakow,' Anton said. 'They will hunt you down and kill you.'

'How many?' I asked.

'Six men. Six killers.'

'I consider that an insult,' Bull said, shaking his head in disbelief. 'Only six!'

Anton ignored him. Probably not been used to much irony so far in his life. 'Tomorrow you will be dead.'

'Then we best make the most of our time,' I said. 'Go on, kid. Go find Mrs Freeman. You have work to do.'

He rose from his chair and with one last look at Bull, headed towards the small office off the reception area.

'What's the plan for today?' Bull said. 'Can I do some more whispering?'

'Pieter's turn tonight. We hit the second pimp. Save the one in Old Cezar for tomorrow.'

'When the killers arrive,' said Red. 'After we take out the second pimp that will only leave the third. Pretty big clue to what our actions will be.'

'That's what I'm hoping,' I said.

It's the waiting that gets you. You review your strategy, your grand plan for the fight to come. You look again at your tactics, trying to second-guess what the enemy will do and work out your counter measures. You clean your guns. You make sure you have all your mojos – the notebook that took a bullet that would otherwise have killed you, the lucky T-shirt that successfully hid your gun from sight, anything and everything, no matter how small. Then you do it all over again. And this was just a skirmish, didn't even rate the word battle. I looked around the breakfast table and picked up all the signs.

Pieter was stirring sugar in his coffee cup so much that it was touch and go what would give way first, the spoon or the bottom of the cup. Stan was making comprehensive notes of something or other on a large sheet of paper, scribbling away and crossing out as much as he was writing. Red had retreated into his Comanche shell, eyes glazed as if in another world. And Bull? I swear I saw him twitch an eyebrow.

'Red,' I said, snapping him out of his meditation. 'Take Pieter and scout out tonight's ground. Stan, you do the same for tomorrow's.'

'And me?' said Bull.

'You hold the fort.'

'And you?' he asked.

'I'm going to give Leclerk a treat. Take him on a little excursion.'

'Nothing too taxing, I hope,' said Red. 'Looks like the kind of guy who'd break into a sweat just getting out of bed.'

'It's his brain I'm going to exercise, not his body.'

'You'll be going easy on him, then,' said Bull. 'Unless your IQ has just jumped by twenty points overnight.'

'I'm hoping to test out the theory that location can be a great advantage when confronting a person.'

'I thought we knew that already,' said Stan. 'Like always make your stand at the top of a hill. Didn't your Lord Wellington say that?'

'This isn't going to be a battle of arms. More like a battle of brains.'

'Good luck, then,' said Bull. 'Sounds like you're gonna need it.'

'Thanks for your faith in me,' I said.

'Don't mention it,' said Bull.

So I didn't.

If Leclerk was pleased to see me, he hid it well. Maybe he suspected what I had in store for him. No, would be too wild a guess.

He was sitting in the lobby drinking coffee and frowning. Maybe the hotel's coffee was as good as Stan's tea.

'What brings you here?' he asked. 'I thought we'd seen the parting of the ways.'

'Everybody deserves a second chance,' I said.

'That's generous of you,' he said.

'I'm that kind of guy,' I replied.

'Get on with it, Silver. What do you want?'

'I'm going to show you more of the local territory. Slip on something casual and we're off.'

He left the coffee and waddled up to his room. He reappeared after five minutes. His version of casual was to take off his tie and leave his briefcase behind. I gave a small sigh and guided him through the door of the hotel on to the promenade. About a hundred yards along was a centre for water sports with everything from speed boats for waterskiing, rowing boats, through to windsurfers, small sailing dinghies and jet skis. I chose a rowing boat, slow but serene. I told Leclerk to take off his shoes and socks and roll up his trouser legs. For a man of his build he had very dainty feet, more often seen on a teenage girl rather than a fifty-something-year-old man. I left him nervously looking out to sea while I made the arrangements with the young boy in charge of the boats. I led Leclerk towards the small boat.

'You expect me to get in that?' he asked, his voice raised an octave.

'Humour me. You might even enjoy it. I'll do the hard work, so what have you got to lose?'

'Only my dignity,' he said.

I paddled into the water and held the boat steady while he climbed in. He made a hash of it and I had to work hard to keep the boat from tipping over. His face was white with fear. I climbed in, fixed the oars in the rowlocks and edged away from the shore. Rowing was not going to be easy due to my left arm being so much less powerful than my right. If I didn't concentrate on what I was doing, we'd go round in circles. Maybe that was an omen for the conversation to come.

I rowed towards the island and stopped a few hundred yards away from the clumps of trees bordering the shoreline. Leclerk wasn't scared any more. He was petrified. Didn't know what was worse – the boat moving along the water to some sort of objective or sitting there stranded betwixt and between.

'What's your first name?' I asked him.

'Claude,' he replied. It kind of fitted him well, I thought.

'Well, Claude, let me fill you in on progress since we last met.' I told him of yesterday night's foray into the world of prostitution. He gave a little smile when he heard what Bull had done. 'You see, Claude,' I said, 'what we're doing at the moment is only small beer. Even if we manage to break his prostitution racket, we'll still just be a tic on an elephant's hide. We're going to have to escalate proceedings into the drugs and arms smuggling. Hurt him bad. And that's where you come in.'

'What do you want?' he asked. 'You already know that my presence here is unofficial. I told you I'd do what I can.'

'Which didn't sound like much. That's why we thought you would be a hindrance rather than a help. If we're going to break Provda, we need you to get proactive. How much access can you get to Europol files?'

'I can access almost everything that is important through my laptop.'

'Then what I want you to do is go snooping through the files. Pick up every rumour, every lead, no matter how small and guide us to where we can do the most damage. You'll be working with us, so you don't need to worry about protocol. You won't need evidence that will stand up in court. I can feed you some names from the spreadsheets, but they will only be the small players, the foot soldiers. See what you can do with them. See if you can put pressure on any of them. We need a time and a date for a drugs or arms shipment. And we need it quick. The forces against us will grow with every day. If we don't put Provda out of business now, we will probably have missed a golden opportunity. Dig around for us, Claude. Pull in any favours you've got. Get us some information we can act on.'

'If I say yes, will you take me back to shore?'

I nodded.

'Then yes.'

I gave him a smile, took one last look at the island with its tranquil greenery, and picked up the oars, started rowing back.

'How did you know that I was afraid of water?' he asked.

'You made a mistake not taking the best seat in the hotel lounge with the magnificent view of the lake. Everyone's afraid of something, got a weak spot, and, no offence, you look like a guy who's afraid of a lot of things.'

'And this is how you treat someone who bought two bottles of the finest wine?'

'You forgot the olives.'

I bumped into Mrs Freeman on my return. She looked harassed.

'Going well?' I asked.

'Came out for more tea,' she replied. 'Thank God for tea.'

'What's the problem?'

'The problem is that he is so stubborn. His initial reaction to anything is to question it and refuse to believe what I say. He's hard to get through to.'

'A lot of years of conditioning to break down.'

'It's not just about improving his English – that, at least, is going well. He's a quick learner. I've been trying to drum into him some moral values, all of which he resists.'

'Outside your brief,' I said.

'How can you let a young boy go through the world thinking that wrong is right and that money can get you anything?'

'We need to disillusion him of that soon, otherwise it will get so deeply ingrained that there'll be no hope of changing him. What does he like to read? Can you introduce him to the legends of King Arthur, Robin Hood, William Tell and the like? Heroes who fought for the ordinary citizen.'

'From what I gather, he has no interest in anything outside his father and his business. If there is something he's passionate about, he keeps it well hidden.'

'Then we need to search deeper. Everyone possesses two things – a fear that renders them incapable and a passion that can consume them. The former I don't care about at the moment, although that may be useful in the future; the latter is what we must find if we are to get through to him. Something that can draw him away from his father, if only briefly and from time to time.'

'Maybe tea will help us get the answer. Will you join me?'

'My pleasure. I appreciate all that you are doing for Anton, and all that you are trying to do. For you, I might break the habit of a lifetime and drink tea.'

'Follow me and I'll show you how it's done.'

We moved through to the kitchen where Ho was busy preparing vegetables for the evening meal. She made a bow when she saw us and pointed to a tray that was already laid. Mrs Freeman brought another cup and saucer and put the kettle on to boil. In the background, Ho was humming some jolly Chinese tune. The humming told me she was happy in her work. Happiness is infectious. If only we could spread it to Anton.

When the tea was made, I carried the tray through to the lounge and we sat down in the deep cushions of the armchairs. Mrs Freeman was 'Mother' and she poured tea into the cups and added a splash of milk. She frowned when I spooned in sugar, as if nothing should get in the way of the flavour of the tea. I took up the cup and brought it up before my lips. And I stopped in mid-air. Mrs Freeman looked at me in shock.

'What the hell is that?' I asked.

'Nessun Dorma,' she said. 'Puccini. From Turandot. It means no one sleeps.'

'Not the song, that's familiar. No, the voice. Unless my ears deceive me, that is Anton singing.'

'And a lovely voice, too,' she said. 'Unusual to have such a talent as a tenor at his age. If it's that good now, it will be staggering in a few years' time when he is fully developed. By jingo, Mr Silver, I think we may have found something to work on.'

'By jingo, Mrs Freeman. I think you may well be right.'

The sky was clear with a bright moon when we left and there was a chill in the air. Pieter had donned his safari outfit – long, sand-coloured belted jacket with a multitude of pockets, in one of which was the bulge of his gun. He had matching loose-fitting trousers and desert boots. If we were attacked by a lion, he was ready for it.

Anton was quiet on the drive to Old Cezar, mentally preparing himself for anything that was to come, I suspected. Stan drove slowly and carefully, even though there was virtually no traffic at that late hour. He pulled up about fifty yards from a set of three high-rise flats – they weren't grand enough to be called apartments – in an open square and we assessed the scene. It wasn't pretty. They were just a mess of concrete that would have looked unattractive when they were built and that hadn't worn well over the years. Chunks of it were strewn across the ground. There were overflowing rubbish skips dotted around and it seemed as if the apathetic residents had used them for target practice instead of carefully depositing their garbage inside. There were red lights in a few of the windows of the flats, and a couple of cars with steamy windows parked up at the open side of the square. A man with long hair swept back in a pony tail was standing outside the entrance to one of the tower blocks, leaning against a lamppost and surveying the scene. He had to be our target, the pimp-cum-minder; who else on a chilly night would be lounging against a lamppost?

'You don't have to come,' I said to Anton as I was climbing out of the front passenger seat of Stan's car. 'Remember what happened last time? Watching from a distance may be safer.'

'You will keep me safe,' he replied, exiting the car with the rest of us.

As we approached him, the pimp stood up straight and put his right hand in his pocket. I drew my gun from the back of the waistband of my trousers and held it pointed down my leg so it couldn't be seen. He was mid-twenties, I guessed, although he could have been younger with a hard life behind him. He was evidently a body-builder and proud of it. He took off his jacket in an effort to intimidate us. The material of his cut-off T-shirt stretched tight over the muscles of his arms and upper body. I reckoned he was about my height, six three or thereabouts, giving him a three-inch height advantage over Pieter, and at least seventeen stones of steroid-enhanced weight. With his heavy build he would pack a hefty punch and be a hard opponent in a hand-to-hand fight. Maybe he would go quietly. Who was I kidding? I had him down as a narcissist who would like to put on a show for anyone watching. On cue, a couple of the currently unemployed prostitutes came out of the shadows and leaned against the wall of the nearest block of flats.

Stan addressed him in Polish and the pimp took a hard look at us, evaluating his chances. The presence of Anton seemed to confuse him – was this simply a business deal of three men blooding a sixteen-year-old virgin?

'You speak English?' I said.

'When I want to,' he replied, trying to sound hard but failing as his voice had an unexpectedly high pitch.

'You have two choices,' I said. 'Leave here of your own free will and never come back, or we'll send you packing with a permanent reminder of our meeting.'

'Mrs Freeman said something about you being noble,' Anton said to me. 'I looked it up in the dictionary. High moral principles, it said. You're three against one. That's not a fair fight. How can that be noble?'

'We'll fight him one on one,' I replied. 'Pieter will administer the lesson. Stan and I won't interfere. Does that sound noble now?'

Anton shrugged, but a smile broke out on his face. The smile told me that he was looking forward to Pieter getting beaten to a pulp by the hulk of a man who watched all of us intently.

Pieter stepped forwards and took his gun from out of his pocket and tossed it to me. He faced up to the pimp and gave him a come-on sign by waving the fingers on both hands. This would be a fight of brain over brawn, and agility was Pieter's best weapon. The pimp walked slowly forwards until he was in range of Pieter and swung a right cross. Pieter nimbly swerved to his right out of reach of the punch and sent a straight left in return. He hit the pimp on the chin, who staggered back a pace. I could feel him revising his opinion of Pieter.

The pimp came in again, this time more cautiously. He tried to grab Pieter by the throat, but Pieter stepped back, leaving him grabbing at air. The pimp tried a right cross, but Pieter grabbed his arm and pulled him around, sweeping his right leg behind the pimp's right and kicking his leg from under him, and he crashed to the ground. Pieter was playing with him now. Anton was shaking his head at the turn of events.

The pimp dragged himself up and approached Pieter again. Suddenly, the pimp's hand dived into his pocket and came out with a knife. Pieter took a step back and the pimp laughed.

Pieter took off his jacket and wound it round his left arm

so that it could be used as a buffer to ward off the knife. He then bent down, fumbled under the baggy leg of his right trouser, revealing a scabbard strapped there, and came up with a long knife in his hand. The light from the moon caught it and sparkled and would have been picturesque in different circumstances. I could see clearly that one side of the blade was straight and would be used for cutting your way through the bush: the other side was serrated and would be an effective saw when the going got too dense.

Anton drew a sharp breath. Looked across at me to gauge my reaction.

'Fair fight,' I mouthed.

The pimp lunged forwards and Pieter deflected the knife with his wrapped left arm. He slashed down the pimp's T-shirt, exposing the muscles beneath. The pimp tried to sweep the blade across Pieter's stomach and again Pieter's left arm deflected the blow. I saw Pieter step back and look down at his arm. The pimp had drawn blood. Pieter would get mean now.

He feinted with the knife as if aiming for the pimp's face and at the last moment, drew the blade across the pimp's midriff. A line of blood appeared on his stomach. The pimp tried another sweep and Pieter ducked under, turned the blade to the serrated side and ran it down the upper arm of the pimp. It was a deep cut and you could hear the noise of the blade against bone. Anton went white.

The pimp advanced again and Pieter parried the blow and slashed down like an over-enthusiastic surgeon on the pimp's right cheek. Blood sprang from the deep cut and the pimp stepped back with fear on his face. Pieter stepped left and slashed at the other cheek. Another line of blood. The pimp, if he survived, would need the wounds stitched and even then they would leave scars as a permanent reminder of the fight.

But the pimp would survive. The fight had gone out of him and he made one final effort at piercing Pieter's defences. Pieter stepped right and made three strokes on the pimp's forehead – they formed P for Pieter. The pimp turned and ran. Only one left for tomorrow. It would be my turn then to show Anton some action.

I turned to Anton. 'Noble enough for you?' I said.

He turned around and threw up the contents of his stomach.

Seems like it might have been too noble.

CHAPTER THIRTEEN

'I'M AFRAID I'VE been rather a naughty girl,' said Mrs Freeman to my astonishment.

I pushed aside my half-eaten cooked breakfast – my heart was no longer in it – and invited her to take a seat. Red moved along one position so that the chair next to me was vacant.

'I've been Googling,' she said. The mystery deepened. 'I've spent some of your money.'

'And I didn't even notice,' I said.

'Well, you wouldn't,' she said. 'I haven't charged you yet.'

I shook my head. This was too surreal for this early in the morning.

'What sin have you committed, Mrs Freeman? I'm agog with anticipation.'

'Well,' she said slowly, drawing out the agony, 'you know we were talking yesterday?'

I nodded. It seemed the right thing to do. We must have talked about something during the course of the day. How could I deny it?

'Well,' she said again. 'I've made all the arrangements.'

I poured myself another cup of coffee to give me time to think.

'And exactly what are the arrangements?'

'The tickets,' she said.

'Mrs Freeman,' I said, 'I'm afraid you've lost me. I think you had better start from the beginning.'

'Anton,' she said as if it would all now make sense. 'Don't you remember? We were talking about his singing?'

'Ah! And?'

'I went on the interweb thingy and did a search. There's a performance of *Carmen* in Krakow tomorrow evening. It's by Bizet, you know?'

'I'm not totally ignorant of such matters, Mrs Freeman.'

'Of course not,' she said, sounding unconvinced that a man of action could be aware of anything relating to culture. 'I've booked two tickets for Anton and me.'

'Ah!' I said again. It was finally beginning to make sense.

'I thought we could go on the train,' she said. 'That would give us lots of time to practise his English and wouldn't be any inconvenience to you. I think it would be good for him to take some time out and, one never knows, it might fire his imagination.'

'It's worth a shot,' I said. 'A new interest might be just what he needs. Well done. Let me know what I owe you.'

'I've also booked a hotel for the night,' she said tentatively. 'There wasn't any way we could get the train back at that time of night.'

'As I said, tell me what I owe you. You've done well, I hope it works out as we would wish.'

She smiled, her confession over and concluded to her deep satisfaction.

'Another thing,' I said. She frowned, wondering, I suspected, what I was going to land on her now. 'I'm taking Anton on a little excursion this morning. Give you a break. I'll have him back by lunch.'

'And where are you going?'

'The gun club. I promised to teach him how to shoot.'

'Oh dear,' she said. 'I'm not sure I approve. I hope, Mr Silver, that we aren't going to clash over his outside interests.'

'Never fear,' I said. 'I have all of our own best interests at heart. You'll see in time. Trust me on this one.'

'I suppose I'd better,' she said, sounding unconvinced.

'I suppose you had.'

Anton and I drove to the gun club in silence. At intervals, he would look across at me and open his mouth and then think better of it. Finally, as we pulled up outside, he plucked up enough courage to ask his question.

'How did you know my father would send his men last night?'

While Stan, Pieter and I were in Old Cezar cutting into his business, Provda had tested our defences. Our Baker Street Irregulars had easily spotted Provda's fracture clinic of an army and raised the alarm by blowing the klaxons. By the time Bull and Red arrived, the thugs had panicked and long gone.

'I thought I explained to you,' I said. 'I can't influence what your father will do and what he won't do, so I have to plan for all eventualities. Your father has disappointed me. He has been too predictable. The more predictable he is, the easier it is to plan the correct counter tactics.'

'Are we going out again tonight?' he asked.

'We have to complete our job at closing down his prostitution business. Can't leave something half-finished. We might as well not have bothered.'

'But aren't you being predictable?'

'I was hoping you wouldn't spot that weakness in my argument.'

He beamed at me. Gotcha, he was thinking.

'The men from Krakow arrive today,' he said.

'How many?'

'Six.'

'It won't be enough.'

He laughed. 'These are the best men money can buy.'

'Here's an important lesson for you. It comes from an ancient Chinese general and strategist called Sun Tzu in a book called *The Art of War*. You would do well to study it. Sun Tzu says that you can only win a war by beating the enemy's best troops. Are these your father's best troops or will he look for better when we beat them?'

'It is out of the question. These men are killers.'

'That's good to know. I won't feel bad now about what happens to them.'

'Mrs Freeman taught me a new word – arrogant. She said I was arrogant. I think you are arrogant, too.'

'It's not arrogance. It's just knowing your strengths and your limitations. We will see soon enough. Then we can decide who is arrogant and who isn't.'

He went silent again. Either he couldn't think of what he wanted to say or he was seeing if he could translate it into English.

'Come,' I said. 'Time for another lesson.'

'You are going to learn me to shoot.'

'It's teach, not learn. And your first lesson will be when not to shoot.'

We got out of the car and walked into the small office of the gun club. Anton stared fixedly at the girly calendar and blushed when I caught his eye. I wondered whether he had a girlfriend, or any friends at all of his own age for that matter. He struck me as a lonely lad, someone who had been thrust into a world of adults before he'd had a chance to enjoy his childhood.

When Anton wrenched his gaze from Miss July, it landed

on the racks of rifles and display cabinets of handguns. His
eyes lit up at what must have seemed an Aladdin's cave to
him.

The proprietor was glad to see us. Hey, big spender, he was
thinking. I swear he was wearing the same off-white T-shirt
as the previous occasion, unless he had a whole wardrobe full
of them. He looked through the round glass of his spectacles
and smiled.

'I've got the silencers you ordered,' he said. 'Arrived yesterday. I've cleaned them for you at no charge.'

No matter how little he charged we would clean them
again. It's our lives at stake and you don't take any chances.

'I need another Glock,' I said, 'presuming you still haven't
got a Browning.'

'Still trying for you, but they're hard to come by. I'll make
up your bill. So that's one Glock ...'

'... a box of cartridges.'

'... a box of cartridges and five silencers. Anything else?'

'Not unless you've got the odd hand grenade.'

He laughed. Thought I was joking. He put the Glock, cartridges and silencers on the counter. I pocketed the silencers
and left the Glock where it was. I took out a pair of the gloves
we'd had made and slipped them on. They were chamois
leather, the man who made them said. They were wafer thin
and wouldn't get in the way of our precious relationship with
the gun. I checked the Glock and picked it up.

'First lesson,' I said. 'This is the safety catch. Always keep
it on until the moment you want to shoot. Got that?'

He nodded.

'Second lesson. You never point the gun at someone unless
you aim to use it. That way you won't shoot your friends or
some innocent bystander. For lesson three, we need to go to
the range.'

We walked downstairs to the empty range and I showed him the targets. They were set at fifty metres, which was going to be way too far for a first practice. I wound one forward to twenty metres, loaded the gun with one bullet – I wasn't taking any chances that he might get a notion to do his father's work for him – and passed the Glock to him.

'In your own time, shoot at the target.'

He raised the gun, pointed it and fired. The gun kicked in his hand and the shot went high.

'Every action has an equal and opposite reaction – that's Newton, not Sun Tzu. You fire the gun and it's going to resist the force inside the chamber. That's called a kick. Watch me.'

I took out my gun, aimed at the fifty metre target, fired and put a bullet in the centre of the ring. Bullseye. Except you couldn't tell that because the dum-dum bullet had shattered the target. What might have been the bull had been blown apart by the explosive power of the bullet on impact.

'What did you see?' I asked him.

'You pointed the gun and fired.'

'How did I fire?'

He looked at me like I was an idiot asking such an easy question.

'You pulled the trigger.'

'No, I didn't. I *squeezed* the trigger. On a practice range like this you breathe out and squeeze the trigger. Squeezing cuts down the violence of the kick. Now you won't miss. Try it.'

I loaded another bullet into his gun and passed it to him. I wound the target forward another five metres. He squeezed the trigger this time, but still missed.

'OK,' I said. 'Try this.'

I picked up my gun in both hands, took a steady full-on stance, aimed at a new target and fired again. Same result.

146

Shattered bullseye. I loaded another bullet in his Glock and handed it to him.

'Take up the stance,' I said. 'Using both hands will steady the gun more when the kick comes.'

He copied my stance and fired the gun. He still missed. I wound the target forward another five metres. At this range you could almost stretch out to your opponent and hit him on the head with the gun. He tried again. And missed again. Whatever his singing ability, this boy was not a natural at shooting a gun. I wondered about suggesting he should have his eyes tested, but thought that might be too humiliating.

We carried on trying. On the next six attempts he scored one hit. At least I had something to give him a little encouragement.

'Well done,' I said. 'You're improving. A little more practice and, who knows, you could be representing Poland at the Olympics.'

'Thank you,' he said. 'That was fun. When can we do it again?'

'We'll give you a day or so to recover – shooting takes a lot out of a man – and then come back.'

'Can I keep the gun?'

'I'll look after it for you till the next time. Don't worry, I won't wear it out.'

He handed the gun back to me and I picked it up like I was afraid it was going to bite me – hopefully demonstrating my point in basic gun handling – and put it carefully in my pocket. OK, the morning hadn't gone quite as well as I had planned, but I think you could still say mission accomplished.

'You're disappointed in Anton, aren't you?' said Bull.

We were walking along the promenade to get some fresh air to clear our heads for the evening and to motivate our irregular troops on guard so that they stayed alert at all times and didn't think the task was done.

'Not everyone can be good at shooting. Although, I must admit he's the worst shot I've ever seen. And, anyway, it takes practice. Granted, in his case it will be a whole lot of practice.'

'I didn't mean shooting,' said Bull. 'You're just not getting through to him like you thought you would.'

I gave a shrug that I knew Bull would interpret as a reluctant yes.

'You thought that if you exposed him to us –and you in particular – he would see the error of his ways. Learn some useful lessons on what is right and what is wrong, maybe start to think about humanity and how to protect people rather than exploit them.'

'I haven't given up yet,' I said.

'No, and you probably never will. But that's a lesson we don't want him to learn.'

'It's early days,' I said. 'We've only had skirmishes so far. The war's hotting up. He hasn't seen our full power yet.'

'Hell, Johnny,' he said. 'There comes a time in a man's life when you have to choose those battles that you can win and those that you are prepared to lose.'

'I'm not prepared to abandon him right now.'

'Then you're taking one hell of a risk.'

'Reckon so.'

The three of us drove to Old Cezar at sunset. I sat in the front with Stan and Anton sat bolt upright in the back seat, eager for the action to start and our public humiliation to be completed. I half turned when he spoke to me.

'Why are there only two of you this time?' he asked.

'Because there's no need for more,' I replied. 'If it wasn't for the language barrier, I would have come on my own.'

'Why not just send Stan in that case?' he said.

'Because I wouldn't get much respect if I didn't do the things I asked the others to do.'

'My father doesn't believe in getting his hands dirty.'

'Is there anything your father does believe in?' I said.

'That the strong should rule over the weak.'

'Has Mrs Freeman taught you the expression the boot is on the other foot?' I said, looking in the rear view mirror to judge his reaction.

'I do not understand,' he said.

'Maybe we'll give you a demonstration so that the lesson will stick in your mind.'

Stan brought the car and the conversation to a halt. We had to park in one of the main car parks as the streets in the old district were too narrow for cars. We got out and felt the evening breeze blow through our hair. I zipped up the light blue jacket I was wearing over a white T-shirt and pale blue jeans. Stan was wearing a similarly coloured outfit and we stood out against the darkness of the side streets. I settled the Glock in the small of my back. The extra length from the silencer made it feel uncomfortable and I adjusted it as best I could without any real relief. Anton walked behind us in our slipstream, looking from left to right for his father's hired hands to appear.

The narrow alleys ran like spokes of a wheel to a central point at the top of a hill where an ancient church stood proudly. The alleys were cobbled and treacherous underfoot. My guess was that the pimp would be at the top – better, if called for help, to run down the hill than up it. The houses at each side of the alleys were tall with iron railings on the bottom two storeys and Juliet balconies for the two floors above. Some had lights on and I could see people sitting in small rooms with old brown wooden furniture. These were not the homes of the affluent. If this was the red light district, then it ran on a very low wattage. As a customer, you would have to be pretty desperate to come here on foot and wend your way through the enveloping darkness – the tall buildings on each side of the alleys didn't even allow the light of the moon to get through to ground level.

We worked our way upwards and came across a working girl. She had artificially blonde hair and was dressed in a pair of black leather shorts with a skin-tight white vest, which strained to hold her assets, and boots that went over her knees. Subtle she wasn't. She approached us and spoke in Polish. I asked Stan what she had said.

'Group rates for the three of us,' he answered. 'We could leave Anton here while we go about our business. Might further his education. Trigger a personality change.'

It was tempting, but I'd rather he learnt from someone for whom he felt affection than someone who gives him an infection.

Stan spoke back to the girl and she shook her head. He took a roll of notes from his pocket and peeled off some. She looked back at him and shook her head again. Stan added more notes and showed them to her. She held out her hand and Stan passed the money over to her. She pointed up the hill and then slightly to the right. We continued to climb in the same direction we'd been taking before we met her. Didn't seem as if we'd got value for money.

At intervals up the hill, some of the residents had opened their front rooms as tiny bars where old men sat playing cards and drinking beer in the gloom. The town sure knew how to have fun. We hurried Anton past and up the hill.

When we reached the top, Stan pointed right and we followed him across a small plaza to a café that overlooked the church. On the outside, there were tin placards advertising brands of beer and cigarettes that, from the age of the signs, had gone out of production decades ago. We went in and faces turned towards us. They inspected us and, curiosity assuaged, resumed banging dominoes on the table and gulping brandy. The air was filled with smoke, openly flouting the law and not giving a damn.

The pimp stood out like a hog roast at a bar mitzvah. He was forty years younger than the rest of the clientele for a start and looked like he had done time in prison. His arms, in a black sleeveless T-shirt, were covered in amateurish tattoos, only some of them obscene. He had a Freddie Mercury moustache and short, cropped hair. He had big rings on all his fingers that were going to make a mess of my face if he landed a punch. He was sitting at a table in the corner with a good view of the door and looked away when we came in. We walked up to him and sat down at his table.

Stan spoke to him in Polish and got a nod as a reply.

'He speaks English,' Stan said.

'Drink up,' I said to the pimp. 'We've got business to discuss outside.'

He shook his head, took a long pull at his cigarette, blew smoke across the table at us. Anton moved backwards; Stan and I didn't budge.

'We could drag you outside,' I said. 'I doubt that any of the other customers would lift a finger. Probably riddled with arthritis in any case. We can do this easy, or we can do it hard. Up to you. How much do you want to get hurt?'

He flexed his muscles, poured the rest of his brandy in his coffee and took a sip. Shook his head.

'You wouldn't dare,' he said. 'I'm staying put.'

'Then we do it hard,' I said.

He looked at his watch and smiled. 'Yes, we do,' he said, standing up.

He walked outside and we followed him. He walked towards the church and that was when I saw them. They were hiding in the shadows of the church. Six of them. They wore long coats like drovers' jackets. Simultaneously, they reached inside the coats.

'There is a time in any battle,' I said to Anton, 'when you have to stand or run. This is a time to run.'

I grabbed him by the arm and dragged him as we ran down the hill. Three-quarters of the way down, I skidded to a halt. I pushed Anton into the cover of a doorway and then entered myself. Stan buried himself in a doorway at the other side of the alley.

'And this is a time to stand,' I said to Anton.

Stan and I drew our guns as the pack kept running down the hill, the pimp to the rear to watch the show. When they were maybe forty or fifty yards away, Bull, Red and Pieter came out of the tiny bar where they had been hiding. We now had the thugs surrounded and they didn't even recognize the fact until the bullets started hitting from both the front and back of them. If the alley had been any wider we would have hit them from the sides, too.

We had agreed a strategy to neutralize them, to aim at arms and legs, disabling them and preventing them from firing back, instead of shooting to kill. It was a slight risk, but we never wanted to take a life unless it was absolutely necessary. Iron fist in velvet glove. And it might be a lesson for Anton. Minimum force to do the job in hand, no more.

The narrowness of the alley meant that they couldn't attack us six abreast. They came at us in a pyramid formation – one in the front, two behind and then three in the third row. Big mistake. It meant that the man in the middle of the third rank couldn't fire for fear of hitting his own guys. The man on the right in the second rank, being right-handed, was blocked by the man at the front. And, on top of that, it exposed the three men in the third rank to our greater fire power of Red, Pieter and Bull behind them.

There was utter confusion; some of the thugs were turning round and some still approaching us, carried along by the momentum of their run down the hill. Our shots made a small, thudding noise as the sound was dulled by the silencers. The three at the back went down first, hand and leg shots effectively putting them out of action. Stan and I shot first at the two in the first two ranks who could fire back. The man on the right we left till last. The hired guns screamed as our bullets hit them. The dum-dum bullets sent sprays of blood across the walls of the alley. They didn't even get a chance to shoot. They went down heavily on the now-slippery bloody cobbles as their legs were shot from under them. We made sure that the pimp got his share of bullets, too. Just the one to teach him a lesson and to make our point that the pimps were out of business – after tonight and the previous two attacks on them, no one would be willing to work for Provda.

Bull, Red and Pieter made their way towards us. They walked past the prone bodies of the thugs, kicking guns away, and Bull added a shot or two for good measure. It was over.

Anton fainted.

CHAPTER FOURTEEN

IT TOOK VOJEK forty minutes to arrive at Stan's hotel. I had predicted an hour, but perhaps the severity of our humiliation of the hired hands prompted Provda into severe-panic mode and act much more quickly than I had expected. Still, we were ready for him.

Before he arrived, we were sitting in the lounge area of the hotel in easy chairs around one of the low coffee tables. Ho had stayed up to meet us, obviously concerned for Stan and, only slightly less so, for the rest of us. She had made a pot of strong coffee for us, a mug of hot chocolate for Anton, and placed a bottle of the Polish brandy on the table with five shot glasses. I poured some brandy into Anton's mug in the hope that it would help stop him shaking. He was as pale as a ghost and twice as quiet. We had cleaned the guns, only then taking off our gloves, and arranged them in a row on the table underneath a cloth just in case one of the guests couldn't sleep and wandered through the lounge. Wouldn't be good for business to seem like an impromptu gun shop had been set up in the hotel.

Vojek looked like he'd dressed in a hurry. There was no uniform tonight, no gold braid to add pomp to his appearance. He was wearing a long, thick coat in a camel colour, a pair of blue jeans, a light blue jumper and brown loafers. He had on odd socks. His angular features and sharp face were flushed. I suspected his temper would be short and was to be proved right.

'There has been an incident in Old Cezar,' he said, scanning our faces to see if there was any reaction. He noticed Anton for the first time and did a double take. He looked away, realizing, I guessed, that he should not have shown that he knew the boy. 'What do you know about it?'

'Old Cezar?' I said. 'Big town a few miles up the road from here. Got a little old district that is evocative of times gone by and induces a bout of nostalgia in all who visit.'

'Not Old Cezar,' he said, shaking his head in frustration. 'The incident. What do you know about the incident? Six men attacked and wounded.'

Six men? The pimp obviously didn't count.

'Doesn't ring any bells,' I said. 'How about you guys? Mean anything?'

Shakes of heads all round the table.

'Where were you for the last couple of hours?' he asked.

'Sitting right here,' I replied. 'Today is usually our sewing circle, but we thought we'd discuss the merits of different handguns instead.' I removed the cloth from the guns. Revealed the line of them stretching out along the table top. Vojek's eyes gleamed.

He took a pen from his pocket and used it to drag a gun near to him and then lift it up. He sniffed it and then placed it back down. He repeated this manoeuvre four times with the same null reaction. The last gun, though, brought a smile to his lips.

'This gun has been fired,' he said.

'Target practice earlier today,' I said. 'Isn't that right, Anton?'

Anton nodded.

'I'm going to have to take your fingerprints to see which of you fired this gun.'

'No problem, officer,' I said. 'Just as long as you fingerprint every one of us sitting around this table. That includes the boy.'

'I'll send someone along in an hour or so.' If he was up and about, then he was going to make sure others in the force would be, too. 'Make sure you're all still here or there will be trouble. And you wouldn't want that. You'd make me mad. And I'm not a nice person when I'm mad.'

Not a nice person, full stop, I felt like adding. But I'd had my fun.

'Meanwhile,' he said, picking up the gun with his pen, careful not to touch any part of it, 'I'll take this. If the bullet from this matches any of those fired tonight, you're in for a long stretch in a Polish jail. And that is not a good place to be, believe me.'

He turned on his heel, took two steps towards the door and then turned around.

'This is a nice hotel,' he said. 'Would be a shame if it had to close. Maybe health inspectors would find some rats or cockroaches if they looked hard enough. Do you get my meaning?'

'I hear you loud and clear,' said Stan. 'I understand what you mean.'

'They might even find some drugs hidden in the kitchen,' Vojek warned. 'This game of yours stops right now.'

'We don't play games,' I said. 'We are deadly serious. Remember that.'

'Oh, I will,' he said, turning his back on us. 'I will.'

We let out a collective sigh when he had gone. It was like a bad smell being blown out the door.

'Why did you do that?' Anton said, speaking for the first time since he had fainted.

'Why did I do what?' I replied.

'Annoy him. Make him mad.'

'Because if he gets mad, he will start to make mistakes. Then we'll have him. Now, drink your hot chocolate. You're going to have to stay with us until the police come to take our fingerprints. You might as well enjoy the time.'

He took a sip and coughed.

'Brandy,' Stan said. 'The first step in us treating you like a man.'

Anton smiled and took a big gulp this time. 'Good,' he said in a croaky voice.

He was as rotten a liar as he was at shooting.

'How do you feel now?' asked Bull, who had been the one to carry Anton back to the car.

Anton said something to Stan.

'Numb,' Stan said. 'He says he feels numb.'

'So much blood,' Anton said. 'I never thought there would be so much blood.'

'Could have been worse,' Bull said. 'We let them off lightly.'

'What did you expect?' I asked Anton. 'Your father deals in a bad world where there are many victims. He's kept you away from that side of things. All he shows you is the bottom line. You never see the hurt that the money causes.' I turned to Stan. 'Have a look at that spreadsheet and pick out some dealers. It's time Anton saw that side of the business. The bad side. As soon as the police have taken our fingerprints, you do a tour of a few locations. This time of night the users will be desperate. Let Anton see their misery.'

'Think I might tag along,' said Red. 'Kinda restless. Won't get any sleep tonight. Never can after a fight, especially one like tonight. Might as well do something useful. You never know when a Comanche might come in handy.'

And so it was to be.

CHAPTER FIFTEEN

THERE SEEMED LITTLE point to going to bed after the fingerprints team had come and gone, so the three of us were
dozing in the armchairs when Red arrived back.

'Where's Stan?' I said.

'He's all right. He's at the hospital,' Red replied.

'Sounds like a contradiction in terms,' Bull said. 'All right
and at the hospital. Is it Anton who's not all right?'

'No, he's safe – in body, that is. God knows about his mind.
I dropped him off at his home when I left the hospital.'

'I think you'd better start from the beginning,' Pieter said,
stretching his arms to shake off the last remnants of sleep.

'It took a while to find a dealer,' Red said. 'The word of the
gunfight has hit the streets already. Everyone is running
scared. Anyone doing anything illegal is keeping his head
down in case of reprisals. It's like *Death Wish* out there. We
went to four locations before we found someone who was still
functioning.'

'Sounds good so far,' I said. 'Better reaction than we could
have hoped for.'

'Seemed to be suiting our purposes with Anton, too,' Red
said. 'With no dealers on the streets, the junkies were on a
short fuse, ready to blow sky high at any moment. Because
we were on the dealers' pitches, they assumed we had taken
over. They were begging us for a fix. Anton was shocked at

how desperate they were.'

'And?' Bull said, one step ahead of Red's story. 'Then it happened, I guess. Someone's taut nerves snapped and Stan was in the way.'

'It was a young girl,' Red said. 'Not much older than Anton. Had a baby in her arms. She offered us anything for a fix. Even herself. When Stan told her what the score was, she went away screaming at him. Came back five minutes later with a knife.'

'And this is where the hospital part comes in,' I said.

'She had the knife hidden in her coat. She went for Stan like a mad woman. I saw the flash of it and only managed to deflect it at the last moment. Cut his left arm pretty deep. If I had been more alert, I could have stopped her.'

'Less alert,' I said, 'and Stan could have been killed. Thank God you went with him. How is he?'

'Waiting to have stitches when I left him. Didn't seem much point hanging around there with the kid. He'd been through too much already last night. Too much since we met him, too. It's building up inside him. I can sense it.'

'That old Comanche nose of yours,' I said. 'Twitching away.'

'Maybe it's a good time for him to be having a break,' Bull said. 'Let Mrs Freeman and this opera trip take his mind off things for a while. We've been pretty rough on him.'

'Too much to do, too little time,' I said. 'I'll have a chat with him before he leaves. Take him out for a boat trip, I think.'

'A boat trip?' said Red, who couldn't swim and hated anything to do with water.

'Location is very important for a discussion,' I said.

'So what's so important about a boat trip?' asked Bull.

'You can't get out of a boat,' I said.

'You know,' said Bull, 'I'm glad I'm on your side. You're too

159

devious to have as an enemy.'

'As long as I'm not too devious to be a friend.'

'That would never happen,' Bull said.

There was a choice of water craft available for hire on the beach. The rowing boat I discounted because my vanity wouldn't allow me to show Anton any weakness, but I rationalized it by telling myself that it would be too slow. The pedalo, too, was dismissed since it would not be good for my image and wouldn't take us far enough out in the lake – I wanted to get close to the island so that Anton could see the whole panorama of the town from far out. Water bikes weren't practical since it's hard to have a conversation when having to speak over your shoulder. I could have chosen the small sail boat, but I hadn't sailed since my school days and didn't want to keep shouting at Anton to duck under the boom. In the end, I settled for the most expensive option – a small speedboat that could accommodate six people.

Earlier that morning, I had taken a brisk walk along the promenade to the designer shops and bought two pairs of swimming trunks, two pairs of deck shoes and a T-shirt, guessing Anton's size as small in everything. When he arrived with his suitcase for his overnight trip to Krakow, I had him change and get ready to go.

He wasn't best thrilled to hear of our boat trip. He said he'd never been on the water before, but, I suspected judging by the pallor on his face, that his stomach had been turned by the events of the night and he didn't trust it in watery unknown territory. I told him it was all part of his education and I wouldn't take no for an answer. He dragged his feet like any normal teenager would do as we walked to the boats and I took it as an encouraging sign. I'd settle for normality in his personality.

I paid the man for two hours of hire of the boat and held it steady while Anton stepped gingerly inside. The man in charge of the boats gave us a push to take us away from the beach and I started the engine. It was a powerful boat, built primarily for towing water skiers and the engine gave a reassuring purr as I pressed the accelerator. We sat side by side in the cabin and I steered the boat towards the island. The sky was cloudless and the air was warm, even with the breeze that blew over us as I increased our speed. I passed him a bottle of high factor sun cream to apply on his lily-white limbs and face. He was reluctant to put it on because it meant he had to take his hands off the seat of the boat he was gripping as if his life depended on it.

'You can let go, you know,' I said. 'You won't come to any harm.'

'What if I fall in?' he replied.

'You've got a life jacket on. You'll float and I'll come to get you.'

He looked at me dubiously.

'I had to rescue Red once from drowning. You can trust me.'

'Red?' he said incredulously. 'You had to rescue Red?'

'He couldn't swim, but there was no alternative but jump into the river from what was left of a bridge that had been blown. Sometimes in life you have to tackle your fears. Although, I do admit that I had to push him in.'

Anton gave a grin. 'Bet he hated that,' he said.

'Not top of his list of moments to repeat before he dies.'

Anton finally let go of the seat and started to squirt sun cream into his hand. As he applied it, I took the boat gently towards the island. When we were about a hundred yards from its shore, I cut the engine and let the boat become idle.

The island wasn't that big, about half a mile long and a

quarter of a mile wide. The beach looked inviting and it was no wonder that people had wanted to come out here and spend a tranquil day. Around the edges of the beach were hummocks of tall grass and reeds – a perfect place for the birds, whatever kind they were, to nest hidden from predators. The grass and reeds gave way to some tall trees, mostly conifers, which rose to a high mound in the middle as if it had been created from some seismic shift in primeval times. On our side of the island was a wooden jetty where it would be good to sit in the tranquillity of the evening and watch the sun go down. It reminded me of home and the jetty by the beach bar. I wondered whether Anna was sitting there at this very moment, thinking of me. I hoped so. I missed her badly and it would have been nice to think there was some temporal connection going on between us.

I turned my attention back to Anton. I pointed to the distant shore of the lake where the promenade snaked its way in all its splendour, and you could see the array of hotels, bars and restaurants beside it.

'What do you see?' I asked him.

He looked at me as if I was mad. 'The town, of course.'

'Wrong answer. Take another look.'

He looked at me even stranger and gave a little sigh. 'OK, the town and the beach.'

'Still wrong.'

'Give in,' he said. 'What should I be seeing?'

'Potential,' I said. 'This place is growing all the time. Sooner or later – and my guess is sooner – it will be "discovered" by tourists all over Europe, maybe even further afield. Wouldn't it be good to be part of that growth?'

'But we would be.'

'I mean legally. Not by running a protection racket, prostitution or peddling drugs, but by going legitimate. Your father has pots of money sitting in the bank – I know because I've seen the spreadsheets. Use it to invest here – hotels, restaurants, boat hire, maybe a big indoor sports centre. The possibilities must be endless. Wouldn't it be good not to have to worry about the police finally catching up with you? Vojek can't protect you forever. It's time to change before it gets too late.'

He gave some nods of his head as if deeply considering my words.

'It would be hard work,' he said.

'No harder than what you are doing at the moment. Must be a big logistical problem running all those people. Keeping control of your empire. And going legitimate could be rewarding in other ways.'

'Like what?'

'The satisfaction of a worthwhile job being well done. Pride in your work.'

'My father would say that pride doesn't bring in the money.'

'Then your father is wrong. He isn't infallible.'

Anton gave me a puzzled look.

'He makes mistakes,' I said, remembering that his vocabulary was still limited. 'Look at how he underestimated us. We're bringing down his organization bit by bit, soon the momentum will be unstoppable. It will crumble about his ears. Quit now while there's still time.'

'He will beat you in the end,' he said. 'He will hire men from Warsaw this time.'

'Can you be sure of that?'

He hesitated. 'My father always wins in the end.'

'Not this time, he doesn't.' I realized that just countering his words wouldn't get me anywhere. 'Is that the life you want?'

Anton gave a shrug. I felt like grabbing him by the

shoulders and giving him a good shake, but that would have been resorting to their tactics.

'This is a turning point,' I said. 'It is time that you decided on the path you want to take. Do you want to be a clone of your father with all that brings? Let's face it, you can't handle the violence that is inevitable. It's not in you. And last night you got a glimpse of the suffering that is caused. Turn away from that course and be your own man. Become independent. Take the path that leads to good rather than evil.'

'Will that make me noble like you?'

'It would be a great start.'

I saw a tear come to his eye.

'I want to go back now,' he said. 'I have got spray in my eye.'

Spray in his eye from a stationary boat?

'Me, too,' I said. 'It's a constant problem in my line of work.'

I pushed the throttle and steered a course back to the shore.

'Take some time to think over what I've said. You have a couple of days away from here and all that's been happening. Maybe even talk it through with Mrs Freeman. You might call her an unbiased observer.'

'I don't know what that means,' he said. 'Unbiased.'

'Come to think of it, I'm not sure Mrs Freeman does either.'

I had not seen Mrs Freeman seem so energized before. She was veritably bubbling over with enthusiasm as she and Anton waited for Stan to drive them to the station for their cultural break. She was wearing a navy blue twin set with black low-heeled patent shoes and a gold locket that she kept fingering in her excitement.

'Mr Silver,' she said, 'I can't thank you enough for this opportunity. I'm sure Anton will come back a changed boy.'

164

'That's what I'm hoping for,' I said. 'Oh, and try not to call him a boy – he hates it. He's not a man yet, so you can't call him that, but lad might go down better than any of the alternatives.'

'I'll bear that in mind,' she said, nodding her head.

'Are you sure you won't find the whole thing too draining?' I'd only had Anton is small doses, but that had been very wearing. 'It's a long train journey for a start and then you'll have to take him for dinner somewhere and cope with him over breakfast and then the train back.'

'I have a contingency plan,' she said with a self-satisfied look on her face.

Somehow I wasn't surprised.

'So what do you have up your sleeve?'

'I've brought along a book for him to read. *The Three Musketeers*. I know the quantity is somewhat lacking, but I thought the sentiments were applicable.'

'All for one and one for all.'

'Exactly. And the importance of having a code of honour to guide you in your actions.'

'Flattery will get you everywhere.'

'That's what I was hoping. Thank you for funding this. I'm sure you won't regret it.'

'We've tried everything else with Anton and, frankly, we've run out of ideas.'

'Leave him with me and he'll come back a changed lad.'

She raised herself on the toes of those patent shoes and kissed me on the cheek.

I reckoned Mrs Freeman would come back a changed woman. They'd have to treat us for shock if these transformations took place. How were we going to cope without the two of them for a couple of days? Life would be Easy Street. But then I hadn't bargained on Leclerk.

CHAPTER SIXTEEN

We were sitting on the rear terrace that led off the dining room. There was the smell of hibiscus in the air, and the deep red of bougainvillea surrounded us like a warm blanket. It was mid-afternoon, the time when Mrs Freeman, under normal circumstances, would have been having her pot of tea. We were in the shade of a large umbrella decorated with the name and logo of the makers of the local beer. In keeping, we each had a bottle fresh out of the ice bucket in front of us. There was a panoramic view of the mountains and their snow-capped peaks and the cable car making its way upwards. It would have been idyllic if it hadn't been for Leclerk.

Trying to be causal and blend in, he was wearing a pair of grey slacks, a blue blazer, white shirt, a striped tie and a matching pocket handkerchief folded so a triangle showed. I was tempted to tell him a cravat would have completed the look – in the 1930s – but didn't know whether he did irony. He might go straight out and try to buy one – if any shop still stocked them. He had telephoned Stan and said that we needed to meet urgently. We now waited with bated breath.

He took his seat and wiped his glasses on his handkerchief, folding it neatly before putting it back in his top pocket. He gestured at the beer and I nodded my head. He opened it, poured a small amount into a chilled glass and took an experimental sip. He raised an eyebrow to convey not bad, or maybe it was just an itchy eyebrow.

'Well?' I said.

'I've heard rumbles,' he said.

'Then you shouldn't skip lunch,' I replied.

He looked around the group. Red took pity on him and said, 'Don't worry, he's always like that. He'll be serious when needed.'

'And that is now,' Leclerk said.

The five of us moved to sit upright and alert.

'One of our agents in the Ukraine has heard a rumour of an arms shipment starting out from Russia ...'

'Where guns are plentiful and cheap,' I interrupted.

Leclerk nodded his head. 'The shipment will pass through Ukraine and cross Poland before reaching the buyers in Germany. A Neo-Nazi dissident group looking to arm themselves, as far as we can tell.'

'How do you know the seller is Provda?' Bull asked.

'We don't for sure,' Leclerk said, 'but it fits a previous pattern that we suspected was down to Provda. You could call it a hunch, I suppose.'

'Where does it enter Poland?' I said.

'It will come on minor roads and cross the border at Chelm. It's a lightly manned border post. Only the locals use it. Any legitimate person on a long haul would take the motorway route via Warsaw, so that adds to my suspicions.'

'How big a shipment and what will it be travelling in?' Stan asked, already switching to planning mode.

'By the size of the dissident group, I would say about fifty Kalashnikovs and around the same number of handguns. Being transported in a lorry carrying automotive parts. Big Cyrillic writing on the side. Won't be hard to spot. Not a big haul, but it would be nice to stop it and pin it on Provda.'

'How certain are you,' I said, 'that you could follow the chain back to Provda? The people carrying the arms may not know who they are working for. Provda would take precautions that the weapons would be untraceable and the chain finish at a dead end. I seriously doubt that you could make anything stick. All you would have done is warn Provda off for a while. Let him know that someone in the chain has talked too much. Provda would simply just postpone his operations until the heat goes off.'

'What do you suggest?' Leclerk asked.

'I have a much better idea,' I said.

I looked across at Stan who picked up a drip mat, took a pen from his pocket and started to make notes. I saw what he had written down as the first item on his list – three oil barrels. He was ahead of me now and had already started planning everything down to the last detail.

'OK,' said Leclerk. 'What's your idea?'

'First, some context. We've managed to kill off his prostitution business and have made his drug pushers worry about their safety, thus cutting down the haul from that side of his business. We're gradually taking his organization apart. Why stop now?'

Leclerk nodded. 'So?'

'The arms trade,' I said, 'is built on reputation. That's what we need to attack. Destroy his reputation, destroy his business.'

'And how do we do that?' Leclerk said.

Bull chipped in. 'Destroy his arms, destroy his reputation.'

'Ah,' Leclerk said. 'I think I get it.'

It was Stan's time to elucidate. 'We need to stop the truck when it gets inside Polish territory. For that, we need three oil barrels and a couple of poles. Block the road, make it look like a legitimate checkpoint. We get the driver and anybody

168

else out of the truck.'

'How do we do that?' asked Leclerk.

'That's where you come in,' I said. 'We need you and your badge to make it look like a Europol operation – searching for illegal immigrants will be our cover story.'

'While the driver and anyone else is out of the truck and out of sight,' Stan continued, 'we disable all the guns – filing down the firing pins so that they won't work is probably the easiest and quickest way. The buyers are going to be real mad when they try to fire them and find out they've been sold a dud.'

'Boy, how the word will spread. Don't trust Provda,' Red said.

'So what do we need, Stan?' Pieter asked.

'We set up a road block with our oil drums and poles. We need uniforms to give the impression that we are police offic- ers – I suggest Pieter and I for that. Bull's too conspicuous – no one would ever buy him as a Polish police officer.'

'I'll take that as a compliment,' Bull said. 'Plus the fact that I'm the only one who could bend the barrel of a Kalashnikov.'

He wasn't boasting. None of us doubted that.

'I stick with Leclerk to translate,' Stan continued, 'and Pieter mans the poles. We wave some traffic through, pull the truck over and the rest of us get inside. Start neutralizing the guns. Let the truck go as if we've found nothing.'

'Provda will never live it down.'

'I like it,' said Pieter. 'A uniform always attracts the ladies.'

'You're not going to have the time,' Red said.

'I can collect a few phone numbers for my little black book,' said Pieter.

'One thing your black book isn't and that's little,' said Bull.

Pieter shrugged his shoulders as if to say, 'What do you expect?'

'But can we doctor the guns in time?' Leclerk said. 'I suspect we can't keep the truck driver waiting for more than ten minutes, before an alarm bell will go off in their heads. Can you disable the guns in that time?'

'We'll use our Irregulars,' I said. I explained our links to the garage and all the young lads who could help us. 'We get them to drive to the meeting point, park up behind the barrier – that would make it look like we were not singling out the truck. Given our number, we might only need five minutes, ten minutes max.'

'So when will the shipment cross the border into Poland?' Stan asked.

'The day after tomorrow,' said Leclerk.

'Shit,' said Bull.

'That goes for me, too,' said Red.

'Can you do it in time?' I asked Stan.

'Seems like I'll have to,' he replied. 'Red, you drive the fastest. Check out the area and find us a location. We need cover so that we won't be seen when we enter the truck and a road where we can stop some traffic – our target lorry and a few others to make it look good – and let others through so we don't cause a traffic jam.'

Red nodded, took one last sip of his beer and stood up. 'How far is this Chelm place?' he asked.

'Close to 200 miles,' Stan said.

Red shook his head. 'I'll be back for a late supper at midnight. Don't bother saving me any dill pickles.'

CHAPTER SEVENTEEN

BULL AND I were pounding our way along the promenade when it happened. Then it was epiphany.

'What does he do with it?' said Bull, without breaking stride or catching his breath.

'What does *who* do with *what*?' I asked.

'Provda,' he said. 'What does he do with all the money? Like it's a cash business, right? Where does it all go? How does he launder it all?'

'There are times when you amaze me.'

'Only times?'

'Don't want you getting too big for your boots.'

'Do you know what size boots I take?'

'I retract my statement.'

'So?'

'Hell,' I said. 'I was so busy looking at income and profit that I didn't check his bank.'

'Better remedy that, pilgrim, or you won't ever be able to hold your head up high when you talk to Stan. He missed it, too, though. I hope the planning of our ambush of the truck has less holes in it.'

We stepped up the pace and arrived back at the hotel perspiring lightly. Bull went to shower, and I went straight to Stan's office and sat down at Provda's machine. Stan had disabled the sleep/hibernate facility and the screen with all its icons shone brightly at me. I had wondered when we first purloined – OK, stole – the machine why it wasn't password protected. Then I realized. It was. But the laptop had been on when we took it and was still on now. Only if we had to sign in again would we need to enter a password. Displaying paranoid tendencies, to be on the ultra-safe side, I borrowed a memory stick from Stan's laptop and copied across all the spreadsheet files. Then I reached for his English-Polish dictionary. I looked up the word 'bank'. I needn't have bothered – it was the same in Polish as it was in English, providing you were looking for the financial word and not airplanes banking, or river banks and so on.

It wasn't difficult to find the detail I was searching for. At least, some of it. There was one spreadsheet with multiple tabs, each one an account. Cleverly, Provda was using several banks with several accounts with each – no wonder he needed to keep a spreadsheet of all the transactions. I had to look up some of the words describing the accounts, but a pattern was clear. The accounts all bore names of predominantly cash businesses – shops, bars, for example. Cash was paid into the accounts in small amounts at a time so that the alarm bells which would have sounded if the cash amount was large did not ring. Then the trail got murkier.

He had set up a sweep system – every time the balance got over a nominal amount, it was transferred out into another account. That was the next job on my list – where was this master account into which everything fed?

There was no other spreadsheet with the word 'bank' in the title, so I was reduced to wading through each of the other spreadsheets in turn. Interesting, but not productive. I found a file containing current information of Provda's credit cards, of which he had many, showing the restaurants he liked to frequent, the suits he liked to buy for himself and

Anton, a couple of expensive watches and air tickets for some future holiday or maybe an exit strategy if things turned nasty.

At six o'clock I stood up, stretched my stiff muscles and walked to the bar to get a stiff, chilled vodka with a beer chaser. *In vino veritas.* I downed the vodka, took the beer back with me to Stan's office and sat down without much enthusiasm. I fiddled around for ten minutes and decided that if one route didn't work, try another. I did a global search on all his files with the word 'bank' and sat back while the computer churned away.

Bingo. There were Word documents a plenty that contained the search word. I double clicked on the first. It was a simple instruction letter to open up one of the accounts I had already checked. I tried another and another. I felt my brain turning to jelly. And then I struck lucky – or reaped the benefit of all the hard work I'd put in. I couldn't believe my luck.

It was a letter to a M. Charbonnier at a Swiss bank – the file name was Charbonnier and that was why there was no 'bank' to stand out in the Word document file list. The reference in the centred subhead was an account number. Strike one! The letter started by complaining that the said M. Charbonnier had not returned any of Provda's telephone calls. Once Provda's spleen had been vented, it went on with an instruction to set up a direct debit for $6,000 a month into the account of a Mr Pavel Vojek! That sum, I reckoned, would convert to about £50,000 a year. Boy, was Vojek in Provda's pocket. Strike two! The letter gave all the necessary information for the transaction to take place – bank name, sort code and account number. Strike three! And you're out.

True to his word, Red was back by midnight. His eyes were red-rimmed and he looked dead beat. He flopped into a chair in the lounge where we were all waiting for him. He helped himself to a cup of coffee from the vacuum flask and a large measure of Polish brandy. Finally, he gave a sigh and slumped back into the chair.

'One hell of a drive,' he said. 'The roads are terrible. Narrow, winding, hardly a place to overtake. Much more traffic than you'd expect for a minor route. Thank God the road was less busy on the way back or I wouldn't have made it for another hour.' He shook his head. 'We're gonna have to allow a lot of time to get there or there's a chance we might miss the truck.'

'Any luck with finding a good ambush point?' Stan asked.

Red nodded this time. 'Half a mile from the border there's a roadside café. It's got a large forecourt for parking. Twenty cars, maybe. We can pull the truck over to park while we let others through so as not to clog up the road. There's cover behind the building where we can hide. Nothing can go wrong.'

'I wish you hadn't said that,' I said. 'Oh, how I wish you hadn't said that.'

CHAPTER EIGHTEEN

THE NEXT DAY was pretty much taken up with preparations. There was a truck to hire, big enough to transport the oil drums and poles. Pieter was to drive this with Stan navigating – they'd switch roles on the way back when it wasn't necessary to give Stan time to think and plan for every eventuality. The Irregulars needed to be given their instructions as to what to do and how to do it: they would travel in four cars, four of them to each. Every one of them would carry a file to deal with the firing pins. We had only Leclerk's estimate for the number of weapons, so played safe in terms of our numbers. Red was to go ahead as our 'spotter'. He would wait a mile back from the border and alert us when the arms truck was coming. He would then follow up and help with everything that had to happen.

Our main stumbling block was the uniforms. They were trickier to find than we had thought. There were uniforms a plenty, but not the right kind. They were mostly out-of-date designs, some going back to Second World War days. We'd had to compromise on what a fancy dress shop had in stock. They were not going to bear close examination. Pieter, being the shortest of our crew, had a uniform that fitted him well, but Stan's was bordering on the risible. The trousers were three inches above his boots and the buttons of his jacket were stretched tight across his chest, such that if he sneezed they were all going to pop off.

I volunteered to drive Stan's car with Leclerk and Bull on board. I'd filled Leclerk in on my discovery of the letter in Provda's files and he was in a jubilant mood when we set off. It wasn't to last long.

We were less than halfway to the border when we got a puncture. I felt the steering pull the car to the right and I lost all acceleration. We slid to a halt on the right hand side of the road.

'It's that hubris and nemesis thing again,' said Bull.

'That's what I was worried about when Red said nothing could go wrong.'

I could see the word 'DOOM' written large in a black cloud hanging over our heads.

Leclerk and I watched Bull do all the heavy work. The wheel nuts had been tightened with a power tool and only Superman or Bull could get them undone.

'What are you going to do about Vojek?' I asked Leclerk.

'Let me have a couple of days to think about it. It needs careful consideration. Remember, I'm not supposed to be here. Let's concentrate on Provda. Vojek is a little fish in Provda's big pool.'

'At least we know where all the money is going. You should be able to sequester their funds.'

'The Swiss don't like that much. Goes against their code of secrecy and security, but we should be able to persuade them when we mention arms smuggling, drugs running and all the rest. I think they will play ball.'

'Don't forget we've got the computer. That should provide all the evidence we need.'

'I'm not sure that will be admissible evidence,' said Leclerk, frowning. 'You did steal it. Could be a problem.'

I was getting a bad feeling. It should have been easy for

Leclerk to reel Provda in, and Vojek in his wake. I didn't like to think of him getting cold feet and letting them slip through his fingers – if you pardon all the mixed metaphors.

'Do you guys want me to mix you a cocktail or something while you're standing there doing nothing?' Bull asked.

'Apologies,' I said. 'Need a hand?'

'No, I'm nearly finished. How much further to go?'

'Around a hundred miles,' I said. 'We're barely halfway.'

Bull gave a groan and tightened the last wheel nut. 'Let's go before something else happens,' he said.

We climbed back in the car and I started the engine and pulled away. Red had been right. It was a bad route, too narrow, too twisty. I went through the gears and had to settle on a steady fifty, and even that with a great deal of concentration. As we drove along, we passed small villages with a score or so of houses. People were going about their simple daily lives, ignorant of what bad things were going on in the big wide world. They mostly looked like peasant farmers with smallholdings just big enough to support one family. A few kept chickens, while we also saw the odd pig. Probably butchered for some grand occasion and cured the rest to eat in the winter. No matter how impoverished they were, I guessed they were happy. Too bad we couldn't all get back to the land.

We arrived at the roadside café on the Polish side of the border around ten in the morning, parked up and went inside to see who else had arrived. It was a small room which could accommodate twenty-five or so customers at six tables. The walls had been painted a dark shade of green that didn't do the place any favours, giving it a claustrophobic feel. Strip lights gave a stark and inadequate light to the place. There was a high counter with three stools where you could sit and watch your food being prepared before eating it. Surrounding everything was a smell of fat from whatever the lady had been frying. I could feel my arteries clogging just by sitting there. There was a sign saying 'no smoking' that was ignored by the half-dozen locals.

Stan and Pieter were sitting at a table covered with a red-and-white chequered plastic table cloth. They signalled the old lady, who seemed to be the only person working there, for a refill of coffee for themselves and mugs for us, too. We sat down on rickety metal chairs and waited.

'The boys from the garage have yet to get here,' Stan said. 'We've got a couple of hours to go before the truck should arrive. No sweat.'

'How long to set up the roadblock?' I asked.

'No more than five minutes,' he said. 'It's not difficult to set up three oil drums and two poles. We can afford to wait for Red's signal that the truck is on its way.'

The old woman waddled over to our table with our coffee on a tray. She was wearing a flowing dress in black under a white apron that looked like it had seen better, and cleaner, days; you could even see her handprints on it. Today was going to be Christmas for her – if she could cope with four of us, Leclerk and sixteen apprentice mechanics. Might even make enough to buy a new apron.

Four at a time, the lads arrived. Stan checked they all had their tools and then went through the whole procedure again. It was now just a matter of waiting for Red's call. Or should have been.

He turned up at eleven o'clock, an hour before we were expecting the truck.

'What the hell are you doing here?' I asked.

'Phone's gone dead on me. Lucky I noticed it. I'll need to borrow one of yours.'

Pieter took his phone out and handed it over.

'I'll get further back to the border post and monitor things from there,' Red said. He pocketed the phone and went outside. Then he ran back inside.

'It's coming,' he shouted. 'The truck's coming.'

We raced outside. No oil drums, no poles. We were going to have to improvise.

Stan ran into the road and waved his arms at the approaching truck. Considering what they were carrying, they might have run him over in panic, but they stopped a few feet away from him. He went to the cab and spoke to the driver. Leclerk hurried over with his badge out of his pocket and waved it at the driver. Meanwhile, Pieter was setting up the road block by himself. Once done, he would then have to stop each vehicle that came along the road, wave some through and stop others to make it look good. Only he didn't speak Polish. Hell, this was turning into a farce.

I spoke to one of the apprentices and told him to go and help Pieter. Needs must. It wouldn't look good, but it was better than any of the alternatives. I told the others to leave the café and hide out of sight round the back till we'd got the truck parked up.

Stan must have managed to convince the truck driver that this was for real, as the truck moved on to the forecourt of the café. The engine was turned off and the driver and his mate got out. The mate was wearing a black baseball cap turned round and looked like he should have grown out of it by now. Dedicated follower of fashion. They went to the rear of the truck and opened it up. Stan drew the two of them out of eyesight of the vehicle and the rest of us went into action.

Bull jumped inside the truck and set to work with a crowbar and a hammer. There were about three dozen crates inside. We had to find out which contained the autoparts and which contained the weapons. Bull levered the top off the first crate, frowned and hammered it back in place. The second produced the same result. We struck gold on the third. Bull threw rifles one by one to me and I passed them to the apprentices who then set to work on the firing pins.

It was slower than we had thought. In the confines of the truck, Bull was having difficulty finding room for the real crates while still being able to access the ones with the weapons. I just hoped that the driver and his mate didn't get edgy and come out to have a look how the search for illegal immigrants was going.

Finally, the weapons had all been spoilt. Now it was time to get them back into the truck and nailed back into place. We worked the system in reverse. The lads relayed the weapons to me and I threw them to Bull. He put them back in the crates, hammered them down and stacked them where they had originally been placed. On the very last one, he had to show off. He took the Kalashnikov, braced it over his knee and bent the barrel into an arc. He gave me a smile and popped it into the last crate. He jumped down.

Now that our task was done, we could see what had been happening in our absence. There was a traffic jam. An old farmer's open-top truck stood there with its bonnet open and an old man peering in. Behind him, nothing could move. They couldn't pass by going in and out of the café forecourt as this was blocked by our cars and the smugglers' truck. They couldn't get round because the road was too narrow. Pretty soon, if we didn't act, someone was going to get irate and start making a fuss.

And then my prediction came true. Someone leant on their horn. Someone else copied him. Pretty soon the whole line of vehicles picked up the tune. We were too close for comfort to the border post. If the border guards heard the racket, they might want to investigate. How much time did we have before that hypothesis came true, too?

My phone rang. It was Red. 'What the hell is going on down there?' he said. 'You got everybody jumping at the border post.'

'Can you do anything to stop them coming to see what the noise is?'

'I can try to block the road out of the border post, I suppose.'

'Do it. Now.'

I told the lads to get back in their cars and leave as fast as they could. They pulled away from the truck and headed off down the road. I motioned to Stan, who was watching and listening to what was going on with a severe frown on his face, to get the truck moving. I went to where Pieter was standing impotently and dragged a pole off the nearest oil drums. He followed suit. The barricade started to be removed.

The driver and his mate arrived back at their truck, checked the back to see if anything was missing – how untrustworthy can you get? – locked the rear and got in and started the engine. Go, go, go, I was thinking. The mate got out and started walking back to Stan and Leclerk. He wasn't wearing the baseball cap. He'd left it behind in the café.

I felt like screaming.

Finally, the smugglers pulled away and Stan could start to marshal all the vehicles in the log jam through the car park and around the farmer's broken truck. I signalled to Bull and Leclerk, and we got in the car and sped away. In my rear view mirror, I could see Stan and Pieter get in their truck and, leaving all the other vehicles to sort themselves out, they dropped in behind me.

'Home, James,' said Bull. 'And don't spare the horses.'

CHAPTER NINETEEN

'MR SILVER,' MRS Freeman chirped the instant I walked through the door of the hotel. 'Where have you been? I've been waiting for you.'

'This may not be the best time,' I said.

'No time like the present, I always say. I'll ask Ho to make us a pot of tea.'

There was going to be no escape. No use fighting against the inevitable. I nodded my assent, gave Mrs Freeman a smile and she strode purposefully across the reception area and entered the kitchen. I took a seat, leaned back in the chair and sighed.

It hadn't been the best journey that I had ever had, and not all down to the quality of the road and the traffic. We'd started with recriminations – what we had got wrong. Bull and I didn't blame anyone for the farce at the border. These things happen. You have to treat it as a learning exercise. What was it the wise man had said? 'Success makes you clever; failure makes you wise.' Leclerk, though, didn't see it that way. He was scathing in his assessment of the operation. He knew more English swear words than I'd ever imagined. It was very plain to see that he had lost faith in us. That hurt.

Mrs Freeman came back carrying a tray laden with everything for a very British afternoon tea. There was the teapot, a jug of hot water for top ups, two china cups and saucers, a small jug of milk and, I guessed, home-made scones. She'd been a busy bee in our absence. She placed the tray carefully on the low table next to where I was sitting, took the chair opposite me and stirred the tea. 'Give it a while to brew,' she said. 'Some things you can't rush.'

Evidently.

'How was the trip?' I asked.

'Mr Silver,' she said, 'you should have been there.'

Probably not, but I didn't disillusion her. She was so bubbling over with enthusiasm that I didn't want to destroy the mood.

'Anton loved the whole experience. He relished the opera and couldn't stop singing on the way back. The only thing that kept him quiet was the book. He devoured it. Had to ask me a lot of questions about what some of the words meant, naturally, but I didn't mind. Sign of an enquiring mind. I think he sees himself as d'Artagnan reborn. Kept asking me questions about being noble and honourable.'

'That's probably my influence,' I admitted. 'Seems like we might be getting through to him at last.'

Mrs Freeman went through the ritual of the tea like a lifetime Geisha – pouring with extreme reverence from the pot into the china cups and then adding the milk. She passed it to me and then popped a scone on a plate and placed that in front of me. She put a dish of strawberry jam between us both, together with a teaspoon and two small knives, and waited for my approval.

'Eat up, Mr Silver. The scones are still warm.'

She gave me a big smile.

Was this the woman we had rescued from the burning hotel just a little while ago?

'You like Anton, don't you?' I said.

'He's a good boy underneath. Intelligent, too. His English

has come on by leaps and bounds.'

'You enjoy tutoring him,' I said.

'It gives me a purpose, Mr Silver. I feel needed, wanted even. I think I can make a whole difference to his life. Lead him to the path that is the straight and narrow.'

'Where is he, by the way?' I said, taking a bite of the scone and strawberry jam. 'These are good,' I added truthfully. 'Very good. We should save some for the rest of the crew.'

'The taxi dropped Anton off at his house on the way back from the station. When you see him tomorrow, perhaps you could put in a good word for me with his father.'

'His father?'

'Yes, when you see him in the morning.'

'I'm afraid you've lost me.'

'Oh, didn't I say? Mr Provda wants to see you all at ten o'clock in the morning.'

'Ten o'clock?'

'Yes,' she said. 'From what Anton said, I think it's important, but if you can steer the conversation round to me keeping on tutoring the boy, that would be very good.'

'Anything else I should know?'

'Apparently, it has to be all of you. He said something about not to worry. It's a truce. Whatever that means.'

'A truce might mean we're getting through to him, too.'

'Well, I'm sure it will all turn out all right.'

'I'll hold that thought, Mrs Freeman, but not my breath.'

I SPENT TWENTY minutes on the phone to Anna and my mood improved no end. She was well, the morning sickness having passed, and she was being sensible, she assured me. Nothing too energetic, that being left to Gus. Trade was good and the sun shone as brightly as ever. I missed her and could tell that she felt the same. This business was getting to me and

I wanted to get home. But if I quitted then, Provda would have won and everything we had done would have been for nothing. I told her I loved her, and she said the same and then the brief interlude was over.

I changed out of the clothes I had worn during the debacle at the border, showered and went downstairs to meet, as agreed, for dinner. I hoped the sombre mood we had all been in earlier would have dissipated, so that we could look brightly at the stage of our offensive.

'All hail the conquering hero,' Bull said as I arrived.

'Very funny,' I said, sitting down opposite him at the table.

'I'm as much to blame,' Stan said.

'Discussion over,' I said. 'Let's order and forget what happened.'

The waitress came and we settled for our favourite steak, chips and salad. She brought a bottle of red wine and we filled our glasses.

'I vote,' said Red, sipping appreciatively, 'that we just think of Provda's face when he gets to hear what we did.'

There were smiles all around.

'Especially the rifle with the barrel that Bull bent,' said Red.

'He wants to see us,' I said. 'Ten, tomorrow morning, all of us.'

'What does he want?' said Pieter

'My guess is that he wants to buy us off. One last attempt to get rid of us and for his business to get back to normal.'

'Then he doesn't know us,' said Bull. 'Waste of time.'

'Still,' I said, 'I'd be interested to know the size of the offer. Just how much we are worth.'

'It's academic,' said Pieter. 'I'm not quitting, whatever the size of the offer.'

'I'd understand,' said Stan, 'if you feel you've had enough.

After all, it's my problem, not yours.'

'I'm with Pieter,' said Red. 'We stick together no matter what. There's an old Comanche saying ... '

'Does it involve dill pickles?' said Pieter. 'In which case, I've heard it.'

'The Comanche say that the strength of the tribe is its warriors, and the strength of the warriors is the tribe.'

'I think I almost understand that,' said Pieter.

There was a pause while we finished decoding what Red had said. When it was over, I turned to Bull.

'And you, Bull?' I said.

'You have to ask?' he replied.

I shook my head. 'I guess that means we all stay. The size of the offer is not relevant.'

Red raised his glass and pretty soon we were all clinking our glasses together in a show of common strength – the strength of the tribe is its warriors. I couldn't wait for tomorrow.

CHAPTER TWENTY

THERE WAS A receptionist behind the desk today. I didn't think she had been chosen for her efficiency. She had dyed blonde hair, a lot of make-up and was wearing a deep-cut white blouse which showed a cleavage that was an advertisement for bra makers for the larger figure – or maybe it was a firm of structural engineers. She was so well-endowed that I wondered whether she could stand up straight without falling forwards. She took in the five of us without blinking. I guessed she was used to seeing thugs visiting Provda and we didn't seem much different to her. It would be good to have an opportunity to prove her wrong, but that was just being vain. She pressed a buzzer, presumably alerting Provda, and waved a manicured hand in the direction of the double doors.

It was like the three wise monkeys. The three of them were sitting behind that big black table in a row. Provda was in the middle in his place of command. To his right was Vojek in mufti – wearing a dark grey suit with blue shirt and tie, and a smug expression like he knew something that we didn't. To his left, Anton. He was dressed in a suit and tie again, and I hoped that all the progress we seemed to have made hadn't been just a brief respite before regression.

'Please sit,' Provda said.

I replicated my stance from our first meeting, pulling a

chair round and sitting as if I was on horse. I rested my arms on the back of the chair and looked directly at Provda. It was important to look casual like we could deal with anything he served to us. Bull took up position to the left of the door, Red to the right and Stan and Pieter leaned back against each of the two side walls. We'd all come armed to cover any eventualities, Glocks discreetly hidden in their usual position at the back of our waistbands.

'We're fine as we are,' I said in response to Provda's command. 'No goons today?'

'It didn't do me any good last time we met. Anyway, Anton tells me you wouldn't take advantage of the situation. Five against us three would not be honourable.'

I nodded. 'So what can we do for you?'

'You can get out of my hair. You're costing me money and I don't like that. Every day gets worse. This morning I had a call, a complaint about a shipment a client has received. It seems the items were damaged. I can only think that that is another of your doings. Needless to say, he wasn't very happy. It seems like I won't get paid.'

'Forgive me if I don't feel any sympathy.'

'Hear, hear,' said Pieter. 'What Johnny said goes for all of us.'

I took up the refrain. 'We made the situation clear the last time we met. Get out or we destroy your business. Nothing has changed.'

'Well, maybe we can get round that,' Provda said.

'Hear, hear,' said Vojek with a crooked smile.

'What will it take to buy you off?' Provda asked.

'You don't get it, do you? There is no alternative. Get out of town.'

'I will go to Warsaw and hire more men,' he said.

'However many you hire won't be enough,' said Bull.

'Haven't you learnt that? I had you down for smarter than that.'

'I could hassle you,' said Vojek.

'How?' I said. 'The only evidence you have against us is a gun with Anton's fingerprints on it. Be embarrassing to follow that up.'

Anton coughed. We turned to look at him.

'I have a suggestion,' he said.

'And that is?' said his father.

'A duel.'

'A duel,' said Provda and I in unison.

'A duel,' Anton repeated. 'These are honourable men, father. A duel is a matter of honour. Whoever loses the duel has to change his position. If Johnny loses, he must give up the fight and go home. If we lose, we close down our operations and go legitimate. There are lots of opportunities here, Father. A duel will settle everything.'

The Three Musketeers must have influenced him deeply. D'Artagnan having to duel in turn with Athos, Porthos and Aramis over matters of honour. It was a hell of an idea. Could solve a potential stalemate or having to deal with increasing numbers of thugs from further and further afield.

'What did you have in mind?' I asked Anton.

He narrowed his eyes in deep thought.

'The island,' he said. 'A duel on the island so that nobody else gets hurt.'

'Place don't matter,' Bull said. 'We'll beat you anywhere. On the moon, if needs be.'

'And the rest of you guys?' I asked, turning round to see all of them.

Red, Pieter and Stan nodded.

'Looks like we have the making of a deal,' I said.

'A good solution, Anton,' said Provda. 'You have become

wise with your new experiences. I ought to thank Mr Silver.'
He looked straight at me. 'We need to talk numbers.'

'Five against five,' I said.

'No,' Provda said. 'That would be unfair. That I have learnt. I need fifteen against your five to make it a fair fight.'

'We'll settle for ten,' said Red. 'Any less would be an insult to the Comanche nation. Any more would be taking advantage of us.'

'Ten it is then,' said Provda.

This was all happening too fast. I could see us being backed into a corner if we weren't careful.

'We need to talk about rules,' I said.

'This is a duel,' Provda said. 'There are no rules. The ones that win are the ones that come out alive.'

'Anton,' I said, 'tell your father the situation when someone is challenged to a duel.'

'The person who is challenged has the right to choose weapons and time and place.'

'Handguns only,' I said.

'And knives,' said Pieter.

'Handguns only – with silencers – and knives,' I said. 'We keep everything quiet. This is personal. We don't want anyone else getting involved.' I turned to Vojek. 'Can you guarantee to keep everyone well away from the island?'

'I'll come up with something,' Vojek said.

'OK, then,' I said. 'The place is the island. The time ...' I looked at Stan. He raised three fingers. 'Three days' time. Dawn. We land on the south of the island and your men land on the north.'

'So be it,' said Provda, looking confident.

'So be it,' I said.

We backed out of the room, walked past reception with

hardly a glance at the receptionist's bosom, out of the building and into Stan's car.

'They're gonna cheat,' Bull said.

'That's what I reckoned,' I said.

'And your plan?' said Bull.

'We'll cheat more honourably than them.'

Before returning, Pieter and Red went off to buy us some camouflage clothing – green for the grass and beige for the sand – and Stan went shopping for a video camera. Bull and I found a coffee shop across the street from Provda's office. We got two double espressos and a window seat. I looked up at the top of the building and thought what a good view it must be from up there. Bull interrupted my thoughts.

'You and Mrs Freeman did too good a job on the boy,' he said. 'Maybe all that honour stuff is going to come back and bite you.'

'Maybe some of Anton's morals will rub off on his father.'

'And the chances of that?' Bull asked.

'Close to nil.'

'I rest my case.'

'We'll be fighting on familiar territory,' I said. 'We've fought on beaches and in woods before. We'll be up against ten city dwellers. They'll be out of their comfort zone.'

'So what's the plan?'

'Too early for a plan. Too little information. I want Stan and Pieter to do a reconnaissance trip. All I've done is seen the island from a boat. From what I've seen – a mound surrounded by trees – I think the key will be the mound. The Duke of Wellington used to say, "Give me a hill to defend and I will fight all day."'

'Attack is easier than defence,' Bull said.

'I'll bear that in mind when I come up with a plan of action.'

'I thought you would say that.' He grinned. 'Be good sometimes to talk like we're not in a movie.'

'Reckon so, pilgrim.'

'Ain't that the truth.'

We looked each other in the eye. Then collapsed in laughter.

We all went back to the hotel and then Stan and Pieter set off to do their reconnaissance. Red stayed there keeping watch. We didn't anticipate any danger, but it pays to be careful. I borrowed a pair of binoculars from Stan and, having picked up our warmest jackets and deposited our guns, Bull and I set off for the cable car to see what the view of the island was like from there.

We bought tickets from the attendant, looked into the control room as we passed and then got into the car. It was an unnerving experience. It wasn't just the height and the steep angle of climb, but the fact that some sadist had designed the car to be completely transparent. Look down at the floor and you saw straight through to the ground far below. The designer had probably thought it would make the car an experience not to be missed and, in that, I suppose he was right, but there would be many who must have regretted the ride once it started. And, in his defence, there was always the fact that if your customers are prepared to throw themselves off the top of the mountain on two planks of wood, or whatever they used nowadays, then looking through a glass cage was probably pretty tame.

At the top of the mountain, there was another small control room with a man checking on those non-skiers like us who wanted to go down, in order to make sure that everyone was inside the car before the door was closed and the descent started. Outside there was a café with a large wooden terrace. Most of the customers seemed to be eating thick slices of creamy gateaux and drinking steaming beakers of gluwein. We ordered two beers. Even the smell of the cakes and gluwein was rotting our teeth. We took seats at an empty table closest to the edge and with a distant view of the island. I trained the binoculars on what was to be the scene of all the action in three days time. I was satisfied. I passed the binoculars to Bull.

'Too distant to see anything,' he said.

'Just how we want it. The security of this duel is vital. Firstly, we don't want any tourists within range when the shooting starts and, secondly, and much more important, we don't want the police getting even a sniff of what's going on.'

'What about Vojek?'

'I don't trust him an inch. He'll only look after himself. Even his paymaster, Provda, will come a far second. Our trump card with him is having his bank records. That means we can put pressure on him.'

'I agree,' said Bull. 'And Leclerk?'

'Don't trust him either.'

'Don't seem to be many people you trust.'

'Only us. And that is implicit.'

'Sounds good, whatever implicit means.'

'Don't play the ignoramus with me. I know you too well.'

Bull winked at me. 'Don't spoil the illusion.'

'Leclerk is a desk jockey,' I said. 'He's a fish out of water, unused to action. He won't know what to do if things start going wrong. Again, our bargaining chip is the laptop – damning evidence against Provda, and that's all he is concerned with.'

'So pretty much on our own, then,' said Bull.

'That's the way we operate best.'

'Reckon so,' he said. 'We've seen what we came to see. Let's get back before I decide to walk down rather than make the trip in that glasshouse.'

I raised an eyebrow.

'I'm not scared of heights,' he said. 'It's the fact there's no exit route. Once inside, there's no way out. I always like to have an alternative or two.'

'Makes sense,' I said.

'Perhaps you'd bear that in mind when you come up with the master plan.'

'I think you've just given me the idea for one.'

'You going to tell me?'

'I like an audience. Let's wait till we're all together back in civilization.'

'Better be a good idea,' he said.

'Trust me. It's a peach.'

We waited until we had finished dinner – a light meal of that delicious wild boar and chips, washed down by a full-bodied red – before going to Stan's room. He turned on the TV and plugged in the digital camera and started to play the video he had taken on the reconnaissance trip. When he was sure everything was ready, he pressed pause and addressed us.

I stopped him.

'Before you start, we're going to need more help from our irregulars. We have to try to equalize the weapons. Provda's thugs will try to sneak a Kalashnikov or ten on to the island. We need two of the lads to camp out and see where they hide the weapons. Then they retrieve them and throw them in the lake.'

'I'll see them in the morning,' Stan said, anxious to make progress before there were any more interruptions. 'Now, down to the chief piece of business on the agenda. The island is basically the shape of a lozenge...'

'What's a lozenge?' Red asked.

'It's a sweet you suck when you have a sore throat—' I started to explain.

'Comanches don't get sore throats,' Red interrupted. 'How am I supposed to know what shape a lozenge is?'

'Think of it as a squashed square or a diamond even,' Stan said.

'So why didn't you say that?' Red said. 'Rather than blind me with science.'

I couldn't quite see how a lozenge was science, but I kept my own counsel. This debriefing could take all night at this rate.

'OK, it's a diamond,' Stan said with a touch of grumpiness. 'Are we happy to proceed?'

Nods from around the TV.

'The island is about half a mile long and a quarter of a mile wide,' Stan said, confirming my initial guess. 'On the south side, our side, is a jetty where we can tie up the boat. It would also be good for concealing anything that we don't want the enemy to know we have.'

'Like the sniper rifle,' Bull said.

'No sniper rifle,' I said.

'Why not?' asked Pieter.

'Because it wouldn't look good to Anton. Apart from stealing their assault rifles we can't cheat – all we're doing there is starting on a level playing field. Yeah, we could pick them off with the sniper rifle, but we have to stick to the rules.'

'Hell!' said Bull. 'The age of chivalry is not dead.'

'It just smells that way,' added Red.

'Sorry, guys,' I said, 'but we have to set an example for Anton. We might just be getting through to him. Let's not mess up now.'

Stan pressed the play button.

195

'Here we are on the island,' Stan said. 'We are walking clockwise – east to west – along the island shoreline from the jetty. Note that there is an area of reeds and long grasses just up from the shore running upward towards a mound in the centre of the island.' A bird came into view. 'These are storks. The island is a protected site for these storks and other wading birds. This part of the shore is wetland – their natural habitat – where the island slopes more steeply into the lake. Could impede our progress if we want to go round that way. Best thing to do is walk up through the reeds, using them and the long grass as cover.'

The picture showed Pieter taking that route. There was then the sight of a headland.

'This represents the western tip of the island, jutting out into the lake. Around the tip is a sandy bay. This is the only point where the enemy can beach their boat and get on to the island.'

The bay was crescent-shaped and looked like it would make a great beach for sunbathing or swimming, if tourists were allowed there. Maybe at some future time they could co-exist. The world would be a better place with more co-existence.

'This shows more of the interior of the island,' Stan continued. A range of trees, mostly conifers, ran up towards the mound.

'Good cover,' said Bull. 'I'm getting to like this place.'

'And then the same sort of scenery back to the jetty where we started. To me, the mound seems the key.'

'I agree,' I said. 'We let them have the mound.'

'What?' said Stan. 'The mound is defensible. We'd be giving them the advantage.'

'Not with my plan,' I said.

'You'd better spill the beans before we lose confidence,'

said Bull.

So I told them, although some of it was still a bit sketchy. Stan could work out the details later, but this was a plan that gave us an edge.

'Always good to have an edge,' said Red.

'Amen,' said Bull.

'But better to have two edges,' I said.

'Where are you going to get another from?' asked Red.

'I'm going to call my mother.'

'That makes me so much reassured,' said Bull. 'Not even sure I'll be bothering with a handgun.'

'Have faith, pilgrim. My mother still keeps a watching brief on the Silvers investment bank. More so after what happened to the American and European operations. I'm going to get her to fabricate some story that allows her to get their banks to freeze the assets of Provda and Vojek. Doesn't have to be permanent – just a week or so will do fine until we wrap up our business. I'm particularly looking forward to seeing Vojek's face when he thinks he's lost all his money.'

'Only one point,' said Bull.

'Yes?'

'Just make sure we're all round to witness that.'

CHAPTER TWENTY-ONE

Dawn, three days later

WE MET ON the beach at the boat rental business at the appointed hour. The sun was just beginning to rise over the lake. It created a crimson mirror on the flat surface – a scene of beauty and peace that was soon to be shattered. Provda handed over a brown envelope thick with zlotys to the boat-hire man who departed with a wide smile on his face. We were on our own now, two armies face to face. Curtain up on the show.

It was a strange gathering. If the sight of Bull didn't put a chill in their bones, there was that of Red – he was in full war paint, blood-red lines running across his cheeks. We were in full camouflage outfit and desert boots with steel toecaps; they were dressed like they were going on a Sunday School outing – suits and ties, unsuitable loafers on their feet. That was their first mistake – they were not taking us seriously.

Had Dickens been there as an observer, he would have described them as 'ugly brutes'. Ten clones of Bill Sykes, but dressed more neatly. There was a varied collection of scars on expressionless faces and a sign of working out in the tightness of the suits over the upper body. There were bulges under the left arms of the suits.

The leader was around my height – six foot three or

so – and his scar was on the right cheek in a vertical line down from the middle of his eye. Let's forget about the others and call him Scarface. I guessed his weight at about sixteen stone, more muscle than fat, a worthy opponent. He walked up to me and tried to lock me with his eyes, hoping I would glance away. Schoolboy trick. I walked forwards to meet him, knowing that my crew was watching from behind me. It was the first time he had seen my eyes close up. He blinked.

'We need to search your boats,' I said. 'Move aside.'

He stayed there, playing his game.

'It would be a shame to get shot before the party starts.'

I saw his eyes move. I didn't need to turn round to know that he was staring down the barrel of Bull's gun. He moved aside.

'Red, Pieter, check their boats.'

Provda, standing there with a suited Anton, had hired the only three small power boats – two for the ten of them and one for us – that the owner of the concession had. I assumed that the amount Provda had paid the man stopped him asking too many questions. Could be very embarrassing otherwise.

Red and Pieter went to their boats and started to search them. We didn't expect to find anything, but it was a good discipline and it gave no hint to them that we had already found their Kalashnikovs and disposed of them, courtesy of the work of our Irregulars. The loss of the assault rifles would be the first surprise for them. Hopefully, the first of many.

Bull and Stan frisked the ten thugs and, having found nothing but silenced handguns and some evil-looking knives, nodded their approval. We allowed ourselves to be frisked and they found nothing that was against the rules of the duel.

One of their thugs went through the motions of searching our boat and found nothing.

I walked up to Provda. He was looking like a man who had

backed a sure thing at the races.

'Happy?' he said.

'Almost,' I said. 'Now we switch boats. Any objections?'

He couldn't say no without giving it away that our boat was going to be slower than their two. He nodded.

We started to get into the boats.

'Is someone going to fire a gun or something to start the proceedings?' I said to Provda.

'I hope the next time I see you will be when you're in a body bag,' he replied. Nice! 'Now get going.'

Bull gunned the engine of our boat and all three boats sped out into the waters of the lake and steered for the island. We gave a smile when the boat that was supposed to be ours lagged behind. Still, best not to be over-confident.

Bull swung our boat round to the east in the direction of the jetty, their boats veered to the west to head behind the island to their landing site on the beach on the north.

When we landed at the jetty, we tied up the boat, jumped out and stood there for a moment, looking up at the mound and orienting ourselves. We had divided up the island into four quadrants. I was to stay in the south quadrant which was centred on the jetty. Stan was allocated the east. Pieter, who was used to being stealthy, had the hard task of moving across the island through the trees and covering the north quarter. Red had the west. Bull, our resident boatman, was to move westwards through the bird nesting site and come down to the beach on the north. There, he would steal their boats and bring them back to the jetty. That would cut off their exit. If they wanted to get off the island, they would have to come to where we would be dug in and get past us. It gave us our first edge. The second was the mound.

The mound was an illusion. Yes, it is generally better to fight from a height. The enemy must approach you uphill, which slows them down and makes them an easier target. But that only works if the enemy wants to attack. We weren't going to do that, at least only to a minor extent. We were going to draw them down to the jetty.

The second problem with the mound was that this particular mound had too little cover. Our enemy would be exposed and we would pick them off from all sides, once we were all in position.

Time to take up our positions.

We split up and moved towards our designated firing points, Bull and Red heading west, Stan to the east and Pieter going ahead to skirt round the mound, using the cover of the trees to take up position on the north.

As I began to move, I heard an angry scream. They had found that the Kalashnikovs weren't where they had stashed them. More surprises to come, pilgrims.

I kept low over the sand and then the reeds and long grass. Once in the trees, I stood up and walked carefully forwards. I didn't expect them to move down from the mound at this early stage, but I wasn't taking any chances. It wasn't easy going. There was no path, since no one came here. The trees were tight up against each other and I had to squeeze into wherever seemed the easiest path. At times I had to take out my knife and slash my way through. Thankfully, the trees didn't last for long. I reached their edge and lay down to survey the scene.

The mound was empty, the enemy having to make a similar journey as I had through the tightly packed trees. From this point I couldn't see how Bull and the others were progressing and, because we were using silenced Glocks, I couldn't hear any shooting to give me news of what was going on. I just had to take it on trust that they were following the plan and not encountering any unforeseen obstacles.

I took out my gun and prepared myself. Nothing happened for a good few minutes and then a head appeared at the top of the mound. One of them reached the top. He had his gun pointed to the ground while he looked around. God, they really were sloppy. I had him in my sights. Shooting uphill is more difficult than on the level as you have to allow for the natural trajectory to take the bullet downwards. I fired two shots in rapid succession. The first hit him low in the right thigh and the second, again low, on his right arm. I adjusted my aim and fired a shot through his right shoulder. The gun dropped to the ground. My next shot went through the top of his thigh and he hit the deck. One down, nine to go.

Suddenly, a flight of storks took to the air and wheeled over the mound, emitting loud squawks. Red and Bull must have alarmed them on their way through the west of the island. Time and co-ordination were now crucial. Red had to be able to give cover to Bull who had to skirt round the west and then head north to reach where their boats were berthed.

A body tumbled down from the left of the mound. Red was doing his job. Two down, eight to go.

I heard the chugging of a boat and knew that Bull was now on his way round the island and, mission accomplished, would then reinforce the south side where they would have to come if they wanted the boats to escape from the island.

I fired off a few shots at the mound, bringing tufts of turf into the air, just to disorient them as to where was safe. The answer was nowhere.

I reloaded the Glock, taking bullets from one of the many pockets of my camouflage trousers and inserting them in the magazine to top up the ones I had fired. You can never have too many bullets in your gun.

Another body tumbled down the east side of the mound and fell towards me. I put a bullet in his left thigh just to discourage him. He lay on the ground, curled up in a ball. Three down. Pretty soon it would hit them just how vulnerable they were on the exposed mound.

It was still for a while. No one daring to breathe. Each of us, good and bad alike, assessing the situation.

They came barrelling down from the mound, throwing themselves to the ground and rolling downhill towards the relative safety of the trees. I fired off a few shots, still aiming to disable rather than kill, but hit nothing. To alert the others, I blew two long blasts on the whistle that hung around my neck. I then retreated back through the trees towards the beach. That was where the final act would be played out.

I hid in the long grass and reeds and peered through to the trees. Red was moving back to his original position on my left and Bull was coming up behind me. Pieter would have heard my signal and would be coming up behind them. Stan would be moving, too. In a moment, both sides would meet and, one way or another, it would be over.

A shot thudded into the reeds to my right. There was no way I could have been spotted. They were shooting blind, hoping to get lucky.

There were only five of them left, presumably two having been picked off by Pieter. The first of them to break cover came charging from the trees with the jetty in his sights. I aimed at his gun hand and put a shot through his wrist. At the same time, a shot went through his thigh. He went down heavily and stayed where he was – the fight had gone out of him, too. He was no threat to us, so the focus went back to the trees. I could see Pieter coming down the mound behind them. I fired off some rounds to keep their attention away from him. They now had my position and gave returning fire. Shots clipped the tops of the reeds a short way to my right. I crawled left about ten feet and took up aim again.

Acting as one, they charged from the trees. Our combined fire was no match for them. They were shooting wildly and taking bullets as if they were that target at the gun club. Arms, thighs, hands, feet – our bullets poured into them. One by one, they crashed to the ground. Scarface dug in his pocket. Pulled out a white handkerchief. Waved it in the air in surrender. We rose from our positions and closed in on them.

Scarface stood up and motioned towards me. He threw his gun on the ground and took out a long thin knife, the type that butchers use for precise filleting of an animal. The knife glinted in the morning sun. He made a come on gesture to me with his free hand. He was challenging me. Man to man. Mano-a-mano.

'What are you going to do?' Stan asked.

'Meet him, of course.'

'Hell, Johnny,' said Bull. 'With your left arm, you'll be fighting him one-handed. Ain't good odds.'

'Pieter,' I said. 'Your knife, please.'

He passed me his lethal double-edged knife. I took my jacket off and, as Pieter had done a few days ago, wrapped it around my left arm as a shield to ward off blows from the knife in his right hand.

I moved towards Scarface. And threw the knife. It stuck him in the left shoulder. Now the odds were equal.

Scarface let out a bellow and stared at me menacingly. While he was pulling the knife from his shoulder, I took out my own knife and walked nearer to him. I made the come on gesture this time. Having extricated the knife from his shoulder, he threw it on the sand and walked towards me.

We circled each other, neither of us willing to make the first move and expose ourselves to counter-attack. Finally, his nerve broke and he lunged at me. I brushed the blow aside

O N E   B U L L E T   T O O   M A N Y

with my left arm and swept my knife across his body, producing a red line of blood across his stomach. He lunged again. I parried the blow, but felt his knife penetrate the cushion on my left arm and cut into it. There was a spurt of blood and an intake of breath behind me.

I stepped back and reversed my hold on the knife so that it was in a position to stab rather than thrust. I darted in and, as he thrust his knife at me, I ducked below his arm and plunged my knife into the loafer on his left foot. Had he been wearing steel toecaps like me, the knife would have not penetrated. As it was, he let out a howl and let go of his knife. I caught it as it fell to the ground and stabbed him in the right foot this time. He was still bending down when I leapt up and hit him on the nose.

His hand was on the knife in his right foot and I stamped on his hand, driving the knife deeper at the same time as taking that hand out of the equation. I made a ball with both hands, interlocking my fingers and brought this doubled fist up under his chin. He was swept upwards and I hit hard in the now-vulnerable stomach, winding him and causing him to bend double.

I had him now. He was wounded in three places, had a broken nose and was gasping for breath. I hit him again with a double-fist move and swept him upright. I finished him off with a series of straight rights and, for practice purposes only, a few left hooks to his head. I hit him again in the stomach. His knees went to jelly and he dropped to the ground, the two knives still pinning him down. I turned my back on him, like a matador does to the bull, emphasizing complete dominance. I stepped back to survey the scene around me.

Those who had made it to the beach were a pitiful sight, blood gushing from a whole host of wounds. Stan and Bull moved forwards, keeping them covered all the time, and collected their guns. I motioned for them to stand up. Those who could, obeyed. Two of them lay on the ground, clutching leg wounds and shaking their heads. Now what do we do with them?

I went up to Stan. There was no way that we could take the risk of ferrying the casualties back to shore – we might do more harm than good if we tried to move them. I asked him to tell the most conscious of the survivors that we would send help as soon as we got back on dry land.

We made the wounded as comfortable as we could and headed back to shore, towing their two boats behind us so that the emergency services had something to use as transport to the island.

Emil and Anton Provda and Vojek were there to greet us. Boy, how I loved the look of surprise on their faces. I turned first to Vojek.

'You have some clearing up to do. Get some ambulances here and send the medics over to the island. Then start thinking of what you can say to get everyone out of trouble.' I turned next to Provda. 'You are well and truly beaten. We had a deal. Unless you want Anton to think that you have no honour, we need to talk about your options. Meet me at noon. Not your office, not our hotel. Somewhere neutral, somewhere public, where you can't pull any tricks. The cable car station. Be there.'

As I walked away, Anton gave me a smile.

'And bring Anton,' I said to Provda. 'He deserves to be in at the death.'

CHAPTER TWENTY-TWO

BEFORE I WENT to meet the Provdas at the cable car, I had Ho, an excellent seamstress so I was told, put a few stitches in the gash in my arm. It wasn't serious, not much more than a flesh wound. I then called in on Leclerk to give him a debrief on the morning's action. He was sitting in the lounge bar of his hotel, drinking Pernod with ice and water, and reading a paperback novel as if he didn't have a care in the world. A little early in the day, but it had already been eventful, so I ordered a beer. It came in a frosted glass. I took a sip and gave him an account of our battle.

'You have done well, Silver,' he said. 'Nearly time now to bring Provda into custody.'

'Give me a few more hours to settle the future of the boy.'

'Agreed,' he said. 'It will all have worked out just fine.'

'Not quite all,' I said. 'What about Vojek? When will you arrest him?'

'Didn't I tell you?' he said innocently. 'Vojek is to be my star witness against Provda.'

I smelt a gargantuan rat.

'And his price for that?'

'We will give him immunity from prosecution. It's a small price to pay to wrap everything up quickly and neatly.'

I was stunned. Vojek was going to get away with it.

'How can you do that?' I screamed at him. 'You're a

policeman, too. He brings the police force of this country into total disrepute. Sends a bad message to all countries trying to fight corruption.'

He gave a Gallic shrug. I got up from my chair, poured my beer over Leclerk's head and watched it drip down his face and across that smug smile.

I stormed out before my temper made me do something I would regret for the rest of my life. Thankfully, I had left the Glock in the hotel, there being no need for it anymore. I shook my head sadly and went out into the warm sunshine. It didn't lift my spirits.

The cable car was certainly a very public place to meet. There was a small crowd of disgruntled skiers frowning at a notice that said 'Closed for repairs' in Polish and English. I forced my way through to where Emil and Anton were waiting.

'We need some privacy,' I said to Emil.

I led the way through the crowd and up to where the cable car was sitting with its door open.

'Let's go inside,' I said. 'We can talk there with no interruptions.'

'I'm not going in there,' he said.

'What are you worried about?' I said. 'It's not going anywhere. Come along, Anton. You need to hear all that is said, since it affects your future.'

I gestured to the cable car and he went inside. Provda hesitated for a moment and stepped inside, too. I headed for the corner of the car nearest to the promenade and turned around to speak to them both. When I had their attention, I raised my hand to swipe back my hair. The cable car immediately moved upwards. We were on our way.

'What's happening?' Provda said in panic.

'We're going on a little journey. Just to get you in the mood for a nice tête-à-tête.'

Sweat appeared on his brow and he kept glancing behind me to the open door. We were too far up already for him to try to jump out.

'Make it go down,' he said, his voice quivering. 'Make it go down.'

I turned to Anton.

'Did you know your father has a fear of heights?' I said.

'My father is afraid of nothing and no one,' he said loyally.

'Didn't it ever make you wonder why someone with so much money would rent the cheapest office on the ground floor where the blinds had to be closed all the time to prevent passers-by seeing everything through the window? Or why, in a place with such terrific views over the mountains and the lake, your father would live in a single-storey house?'

Anton looked at his father questioningly. 'Is it true?'

'Shut up,' said Provda. 'Make him get me down. You're his friend. Ask him to do it.'

The cable car trundled upwards and came to a stop just short of the upper station. The doors were still open. The view through the bottom of the car was endless. Provda didn't know where to look.

'Take me down,' he shouted at me. 'Please take me down.'

'Is he still your hero?' I asked Anton. 'As he stands here begging?'

Anton just looked at his father in bewilderment.

'He was cheating at the duel, too,' I said. 'They had hidden Kalashnikovs on the island, but not well enough so that we couldn't find them. Ten against five and he still needed to cheat. Where is the honour in that?'

'Is it true, Father? Did you cheat?'

Provda had no answer. All his mind was focused on his terror.

'Maybe if we get nearer the door, it would help your father

209

tell the truth.'

I got hold of Provda's arm and started to drag him towards the gaping hole that was the door.

He jumped back out of my reach. Stared at me with hatred in his eyes. He dug a hand in his trouser pocket and pulled out a gun. Aimed it at me and screamed, 'Take me down now.'

'No, Father. This is wrong. You broke your word. The duel was supposed to finish everything with honour so that we could move on. Change our ways. But you didn't change yours. You broke a promise. That's not right.'

'Shut up, boy,' he shouted.

I rushed him. Had to get the gun from him before he shot me. I was close, but not close enough, when the shot rung out.

There's always a delay before the pain starts. Adrenaline works as a numbing agent. I could feel warm, sticky blood on my fingertips. And then I realized it wasn't mine. Provda slid out of my grasp and down to the floor. I looked across the cable car to Anton. He was standing there, petrified by shock. He had the Glock in his hand. The bloody Glock that Vojek had taken for fingerprints. There was a wisp of smoke coming from the barrel. Anton passed out.

I pressed the button on my mobile to connect with Bull. 'Get us down fast,' I shouted. 'And get an ambulance.'

When you've seen as much death as we had, you recognize the signs all too easily. Provda was way dead before we even got back to the ground. He had a hole in his chest dead centre over his heart. There was no breath coming from his mouth, only a trickle of blood from the internal injuries.

My certainty of his death was matched by the uncertainty of its manner. Had Anton simply fired, maybe even just to warn, or had he taken deliberate aim? If he had aimed, he was such a bad shot it was unclear whether he was trying to shoot me or his father. I wanted it to be the former, if only for his mental state in the future.

Bull was still at the top of the mountain, stuck there until the next journey up and down. Red, Pieter and Stan were waiting as we landed. The two operators we had bribed to let us run the car for one journey would probably be in a lot of trouble and for that I was sorry. Maybe we could concoct a story about acting for Leclerk and it was all officially for a good cause, although my new relationship with Leclerk wasn't going to help matters. The signs were gone, but the crowd was bigger now. There was a ripple of excitement among the spectators.

Pieter and Stan carried Provda out of the car and examined him. Pieter took his jacket off and covered Provda's head. Red and I carried Anton out and laid him on the floor where he wouldn't be able to see his father when he came out of his faint. I called for some water and one of the skiers gave me a bottle. I poured half of it over Anton's face and saved the rest for him to drink. The water brought him round and he looked up at me.

'We have to talk,' I said. 'The police will be here soon and we need to tell them a story. Understand?'

He nodded.

'This is what happened. We took the trip on the cable car because in all his time here, your father had not been to the top of the mountain. He couldn't handle the height. He wasn't himself anymore. He pulled out a gun and threatened to fire it. You thought he would kill both of us in his panic. He wasn't thinking rationally. So you shot him in self-defence. You were carrying the gun to return it to Vojek as you didn't want it. Repeat it back to me.'

He wasn't word perfect, but it might just be credible. Who would believe that such a devoted son would kill his own father? That was our only hope.

CHAPTER TWENTY-THREE

I WAS SIX hours at the police station, telling my story to increasingly senior officers. I would have been there longer, I'm sure, if Stan hadn't arranged for a hotshot lawyer to defend my rights (which appeared to be few). The lawyer also attended the interview with Anton and stuck to the line on self-defence. The only good part of being there was when they deigned to give me a cup of coffee. The policeman who went to get it left the interview room door open. As I looked out, I saw Vojek being led along the corridor in handcuffs. I caught his eye and gave him a salute and a smile. He scowled back. The death of Provda meant that his evidence was no longer needed and his immunity was revoked. At least something positive had come out of the day.

The hotshot lawyer badgered the police for Anton's release, pending trial into the custody of a responsible adult. For some strange reason I didn't fit. Maybe it was that my home was a few thousand miles away, but I suspect the fact that I had a penchant for guns and for using them didn't help my case much. So, with all of my crew, including Stan, the local of our group, being disqualified for similar reasons, guess who we settled on?

Mrs Freeman flung her arms around Anton when we came out of the police station. She hugged him so tight that it was probably difficult for him to breathe, but the hug and the comfort it gave was the thing he most needed.

When we were driving back to the hotel, me in the front with Stan, Mrs Freeman holding Anton tight in the back, she asked a very important question of me.

'Has he cried yet?' she said.

'No,' I replied. 'I don't think anything has really sunk in yet.'

'He has to get it out of his system if we are going to help him get over what he has done. Give me some time and space with him when we get back.'

'Take as long as you want. Our work here is done, but we'll stay on until you're sure Anton doesn't need us anymore.'

When we arrived back, Mrs Freeman took Anton off to her room and the rest of us assembled at a table in the garden. None of us had remembered that you could see the cable car from there. I gave a shudder.

'It was supposed to be so easy,' I said. 'Take advantage of Provda's fear of heights to wring every last concession out of him. Go legitimate and let the boy have a life of his own. Hell! What a mess.'

'You weren't to know he was armed,' Bull said. 'And who would dream that the boy was carrying a gun? It's Vojek's fault that the boy had the Glock.'

'But,' I said, 'it's our fault that we treat the guns so casually, like it's the next thing to do after putting your trousers on in the morning.'

'What do you mean *after*?' said Bull.

I ignored him, but not his effort to cheer me up.

'Anton wanted to be like us,' I continued. 'Noble and honourable. I need to take some share of the blame. Didn't turn out to be good mentor after all.'

'Don't beat yourself up,' said Pieter. 'None of us are what you could call excellent role models. What we did, we did because we thought it was the best for the boy and for everyone else around here. We cleaned up this town and that's something we should all be proud of. The boy learned some valuable lessons from our moral code. That will see him right for whatever pitfalls he meets in his future life.'

'The Comanches have a saying,' chipped in Red. 'Act with honour and you will never be ashamed of your actions. You will earn respect from others and from yourself.'

'The Poles have a saying, too,' said Stan. 'If you can leave the world a better place by your actions, then you will die a proud man.'

'Amen to that,' said Bull. 'My old grandpappy had a saying.'

He paused to heighten the drama.

'What did he say?' said Stan.

'He used to say,' said Bull, 'that when all else fails...'

He paused again.

'What did he say?' asked Pieter. 'When all else fails, what?'

'Get drunk,' said Bull.

Which we did.

I woke up to the sound of a hundred blacksmiths making horseshoes inside my brain. I was tempted to make a pledge never to touch alcohol again, but I knew that by noon my determination would be eroded. I went into the bathroom, drank a pint or two of water from the tap and got in the shower. I turned it onto cold and stood there for five minutes, beating the hangover into submission. I shaved, dressed and went down to breakfast. There wasn't much conversation going on, and what little there was was delivered in whispers.

'Anyone seen Mrs Freeman and Anton?' I asked.

'Don't think so,' said Red. 'But I'm not sure my eyes are functioning well enough to see them, even if they were sitting at the next table.'

'What do you want us to do today?' asked Stan.

'Red needs to go to the garage and thank everyone there for their help. We couldn't have done it all without them. Give them a big cheque, too, to secure their future.'

'And the rest of us?' said Pieter. 'Personally, I don't think I'm going to be much use for the next few hours.'

'Don't worry,' I said. 'What I've got planned isn't strenuous.'

'And what is that?' said Bull.

'We're going to start a protection racket.'

When I arrived back at the hotel, there was a note waiting for me at the reception desk. It was from Mrs Freeman, asking if she and Anton could join us for dinner. I wrote a reply saying we would be absolutely delighted, suggested eight o'clock, and pushed it underneath the door of her room. It seemed like it was a good sign, although I still crossed my fingers.

I had a word with the others and said that this could be our last night here and a memorable occasion, and that we should dress as smartly as our wardrobe allowed. I asked Stan to open at least three bottles of the finest red wine he had in his cellar – a large rack in the kitchen, actually – so that they had time to breathe. Maybe a fine, chilled white for Mrs Freeman, too. He asked if he should prepare a special menu and, recollecting the fare on the first night, settled for the safety of his juiciest steaks for the five of us and whatever Mrs Freeman and Anton fancied from his à la carte menu.

The five of us met up at seven in the lounge and ordered some drinks. I'd been drinking too much beer lately and, watchful of my shape, went back to my low-calorie option of vodka with fresh orange juice. The juice made me feel good about the vodka. Nutrition is important.

We scrubbed up nicely, although I thought Red's fringed buckskin jacket was perhaps too formal for the occasion.

We took our drinks outside and sat on the wall dividing the promenade from the beach, and looked out over the lake.

'I'll be kind of sad to leave here,' said Red.

'I've been away too long,' said Bull. 'As I get older, I find that I miss my family and my home comforts more. Be good to be ordinary again, you know? Living like ordinary people. Not always on the alert for danger.'

'Really,' I said. 'It's a habit I've never been able to break. Even on St Jude, I find myself alert to any trouble that might be around the corner. If some of the young guests staying at the hotel get a bit rowdy on a stag night, I find myself planning what to do if the situation gets out of hand. And that's why you, Bull, keep a shotgun hidden in the engine compartment of your boat and I keep a Browning Hi-Power handgun taped under the counter of the bar.'

'I suppose you're right,' said Bull. 'Maybe I'm fantasizing an ideal without recognizing I don't fit into it.'

'We never fit anywhere,' said Pieter. 'I don't manage too bad on the safaris, but that's only because my job is to look out for danger and negate it if it happens.'

'Wow!' I said. 'This is getting too deep for me. We're good at what we do. Not many people can say that.'

'I agree,' said Stan. 'I just wish we didn't have to do it quite so often.'

'It's the leaping over tall buildings in a single bound that gets me,' said Red.

Bull gave a snigger. Stan got out his mobile phone and pressed a button.

'What are you doing?' I asked.

'Ordering another round of drinks. Owner's privilege,' he said. 'I never get tired of this view. I'm going to miss you guys. Things will be quiet round here.'

'Quiet's good,' said Bull. 'World would be a better place

with more quiet. Give people more of a chance to think. About themselves and others.'

Ho came out with a tray of drinks and passed them around. I took a sip. Boy, was this Polish vodka good. The sun began to set. A perfect reflection shimmered over the still water of the lake. Everything almost perfect.

We finished our drinks just as the sun dipped below the horizon and went inside. The dining room was busy. There was laughter in the air. Children giggled and parents beamed with satisfaction. We were just about to sit when Mrs Freeman and Anton came in. She was wearing a deep blue dress with black patent shoes and a string of pearls around her neck. She looked classy. Anton had on a pair of dark blue chinos with a pale blue shirt with a button down collar. They looked like they had made a conscious decision to dress to complement each other. Or maybe there was synchronicity going on between them. I hoped for the latter.

I gestured at Mrs Freeman and Anton to sit opposite me and the rest of the gang took their seats. There was a bottle of chilled white wine in the centre of the table and I poured a glass for Mrs Freeman. She took a sip and nodded her approval. Stan circulated with the red wine and paused before Anton.

'Do you want a small glass?' I said.

He smiled. 'Yes, please, Johnny.'

He looked at Mrs Freeman.

'What have I taught you? Yes, please, who?

'Sorry,' Anton said. 'Yes, please, Mr Silver.'

He tried the wine and pulled a face. 'Good,' he said.

'You'll appreciate it more when you get used to it,' I said.

'Like you men,' Mrs Freeman said. 'We are very lucky to have friends like you.'

'And we'll be better friends if we drop the Mrs Freeman

stuff,' I said. 'Time to tell us your first name.'

She hesitated. 'Evadne,' she said.

'Evadne!' exclaimed Bull.

'Why do you think I insist on being called Mrs Freeman?' she said with a smile.

'What would you like to eat?' I said, passing two menus across the table.

'What are you having?' Anton asked.

'Steak, very rare, chips and salad,' I replied.

'I'll have that,' he said, putting the menu down.

'And I'll have the trout,' said Mrs Freeman. 'And no jokes about old trout.'

'I wouldn't dream of it,' I said. 'How are you both doing?'

'Anton is making good progress. We've had a long talk and opened up the escape valve on his emotions.'

'Catharsis,' said Bull.

'Catharsis?' Mrs Freeman said.

'I get the big words from him,' Bull said, gesturing at me.

'Anton and I have come to a decision,' she said. I crossed my fingers underneath the table. 'I am going to apply to be his legal guardian. The lawyer, bearing in mind Anton's age and the circumstances, thinks he can convince a jury that it was self-defence.'

I gave a wide smile.

'That's terrific news,' I said. 'On both fronts.'

'It's not going to be easy,' she said. 'He will have to go back to school, maybe even university after that, if he works hard enough.'

'Will you stay around here?' Stan asked. 'I can always find room for the two of you.'

'No,' she said. 'We will move to Krakow where he can get a good school and singing lessons – we need to nurture that talent.' She looked directly at me. 'I assume,' she said, 'that

Anton won't get any money from his father's estate.'

'It will almost certainly be confiscated,' I said.

'Then I will need to get a job,' she said. 'I'll go back into teaching. Hopefully, it will be sufficient for both of us to live on.'

I reached under the table and passed the plastic shopping bag across the table to her.

'We had a collection,' I said. 'All the local businesses. That will help you get started.'

She looked in the bag. It contained large denomination zloty banknotes.

'We would also like to contribute,' I said. I handed her an envelope. 'Inside you'll find a cheque from each of us.'

She looked inside the envelope. A tear came into her eye.

'I couldn't possibly accept,' she said.

'We insist,' Bull said. The others nodded their agreement. 'And you know what happens when we get insistent.'

'Heads roll,' she said.

'Bingo,' said Bull.

'Are you happy with this arrangement?' I asked Anton.

'Yes, sir,' he said. 'I feel lost. I hope Mrs Freeman can help me find myself.'

How this boy had grown up in just a couple of action-packed weeks.

'I think we can stop calling you boy,' I said.

He started to cry. 'But how can I be a man when I keep crying?'

'A long while ago,' Bull said. 'We were doing a job in Zimbabwe. We came across some boys about your age. We killed them before we realized how young they were – not that that would have made any difference under the circumstances. That night, I cried myself to sleep. Ain't nothing wrong with a man crying. Does you good to let your feelings show sometimes.' He gave Anton a serious look. 'And if you tell anyone about that, I'll kick you so hard you'll finish up in the next country.'

Anton smiled. He got up and walked round the table to where Bull was sitting. He gave him a big hug. He repeated this with each of us, and didn't hold back the tears.

'I think Anton shows good sense,' Mrs Freeman said.

She got up and kissed each of us in turn on the cheek.

'Isn't it strange how life turns out,' she said. 'A few weeks ago I had nothing to look forward to. I didn't have a clue as to what to do with the rest of my life. And then I meet you men. You've changed everything for me. How can I ever thank you?'

'Look after Anton and teach him good values. That's all we ask. And make us a proper pot of tea when we next come.'

'And some of those scone things,' said Red.

'Ah, here come our bloody steaks,' I said.

'Mr Silver!' she said, horrified. Then she gave me a smile. 'And lots of bloody chips!'

CHAPTER TWENTY-FOUR

St Jude, two days later

BULL AND I stepped off the boat and walked along the beach, our bergans hanging heavy on our backs. As we approached the beach bar, I could see Anna and Mai Ling sitting in the shade, waiting for us. It seemed like an age since I had seen Anna and I had missed her terribly, and it would have been even more so if there hadn't been so much on my mind.

We threw our bergans on the sand and hugged our loves. Bull lifted the tiny Mai Ling off the sand and swung her around in his happiness. I squeezed Anna tight and then stepped back to look at her in all her beauty. The bump in her tummy was visibly larger and I hoped that all was progressing well.

'Did it all work out OK?' she asked.

'Yes,' I replied. 'Not always to plan, but the result turned out as good as we had hoped.'

'And will you go away again?'

'No.'

'Not unless it is a matter of honour?'

'Not unless it is a matter of honour.'

'I understand,' she said. 'Honour is very important to you.'

'I'm a lucky man that you understand me so well.'

'And I'm a lucky woman to have someone as honourable as

you.' She paused. 'By the way,' she said matter-of-factly. 'I had a scan while you were away.'

'Nothing wrong, I hope?'

'They made a mistake with the first scan.'

My heart dropped.

'It's going to be twins.'

Gulp.